STAR TREK 35:
THE PROMETHEUS DESIGN

D1079388

STAR TREK NOVELS

STAR TREK: THE NEXT GENERATION NOVELS

STAR TREK GIANT NOVELS

A *STAR TREK*® NOVEL

THE PROMETHEUS DESIGN

SONDRA MARSHAK & MYRNA CULBREATH

TITAN BOOKS

LONDON

STAR TREK 35: **THE PROMETHEUS DESIGN**
ISBN 1 85286 284 X

Published by
Titan Books Ltd
58 St Giles High St
London WC2H 8LH

First Titan Edition May 1990
10 9 8 7 6 5 4 3 2 1

British edition by arrangement with Pocket Books, a division of
Simon & Schuster, Inc., Under Exclusive License from
Paramount Pictures Corporation, The Trademark Owner.

Printed and bound in Great Britain by Cox and Wyman Ltd,
Reading, Berkshire.

*For Albert Nessim Hassan
and in memory of his parents
Maurice and Regina Hassan*

Prologue

The fire-presence tuned the precognon. Mists of thought and the flow of time meshed to show four small lives at a fire in a crystal cave.

"Both species are young," the fire-presence said, "but of some interest. The divided one, V-Two, spans both worlds. It will state the problem:

"Prometheus brought fire to man and for his reward was chained to a rock to be eaten by vultures. What is disquieting is that intelligent life forms all over the galaxy understand that legend—both the fire-bringing and the vultures."

"Sublevel One, analysis of content—analogy of our research problem to the ancient legend of the subject's Human half-world," the cool one said. "Sublevel Two indicates understanding of irony. Sublevel Three: Does the level of thought indicate a possible advanced Level One concept?"

"Unlikely," the fire-presence said. "However, the subject is the anomalous, potentially outside-the-maze radical subject, V-Two. It is atypical. It is a half-breed. We have tagged it for longitudinal lifetime study with special emphasis on its nonstandard cross-connects with other individuals, which are unusual."

"Its thought will continue?"

"If it lives."

The forward probability construction continued in the mists of time. The dark-haired, pointed-eared younger V spoke in the crystal cave:

"There is both the god in man, which reaches for fire and stars, and that black-dark streak which steals the fire to make chains, exacts a price from the fire-bringer—and lets loose the dogs of war and the vultures of destruction. There is the greatness and the callousness. Nor are we alone in that duality—your species or mine. Every solution to the Promethean flaw that intelligent life in the galaxy has found is, at best, partial. It is also . . . temporary. Nevertheless, it is our solution."

"Forward construction of thought level does rate advanced Level One," the cool one said. "That is unknown in these subjects. The out-of-maze subject V-Two has subject-to-subject designation?"

"Spock of Vulcan."

"Now project a similar level of forward construction for the other out-maze radical, V-One."

The projection swirled and shifted to another scene. It appeared to be on a primitive star travel ship. The older Vulcan, V-One, spoke:

"The essence of the classic double-blind experimental design is that neither the subjects nor the experimenters who manipulate or observe them shall know which subjects are in the experimental group and which are the controls. It is the only scientific design that defeats the illogical susceptibility of intelligent beings to placebo effects and terminal self-delusion. That is not, however, of much consolation to the control subject who dies while the experimental group gets the real cure for cancer. Nor to those killed by false cures. The price of the fire has always come high."

8

"V-One has also previously demonstrated some possibility of Level One, has it not?"

"For ten of its planet revolution time spans."

"Now project V-Two's atypical cross-connects with his H Primaries, and the effect of the introduction of V-One?"

The scene widened to show the H subject—fair, smaller than the two Vulcans, yet clearly a commanding presence. Behind him stood yet another H male, dark of hair and blue of eye, his vibrations supportive, nurturing. They spoke:

H Primary One:	Then—we are the subjects?
H Primary Two:	Or—the controls.
V-One:	Both. And such 'experimenters' as we have reached are as blind as we about which worlds serve what purpose. The grand design is elsewhere —and the Designers yet unknown.
V-Two:	However, the Designers must also have some blind spot. Callousness is always blind. There must be something that we could use—a third blind . . .
H Primary One:	Spock, you've hit it! Gentlemen, do you remember the story about the rats who trained the psychologists . . . ?

"Extrapolation indicates a pronounced 'observer effect,'" the cool one said. "The subjects have detected much of the experimental design and conceived a plan to confront it. If the subjects know that much, will it not affect the experiment?"

"That has been taken into account," the fire-presence said. "No subject on all the experimental and control worlds has yet correctly formulated the experimental design question: Is there some fatal flaw in the design of intelligent life as such—and if so, can it be separated from the greatness . . . ?"

"And if these subjects should succeed in doing so?"

"Then it will be time for the 'psychologists' to interview the 'rats.' "

"This group of little ones is quite interesting."

"It is not a group. They have not yet met V-One." The fire-presence turned to the First-Among for decision.

"I concur in the design," the First-Among said. "Initiate test to destruction."

"It is begun," the fire-presence said.

THE H PRIMARY ONE SUBJECT WAS DIS-ORIENTED. IT HEARD VOICES THAT HAD NOT YET SPOKEN. IT REMEMBERED THE FUTURE AND FORGOT THE PAST. ITS JUDG-MENT WAVERED IN THE FACE OF PRESENT SHOCK AND FUTURE NIGHTMARE. IT RAN— AND DID NOT KNOW WHETHER IT RAN FROM DANGER OR INTO IT....

PICK UP H PRIMARY ONE SUBJECT FOR FULL BODY-BRAIN PROCESSING....

The order went out, completing the pattern which had already begun.

Chapter One

Captain James T. Kirk angled his horns menacingly and bluffed out a devil-horned Helvan who tried to bar his way. Without pause he ducked past and around a corner, out of sight of the horned crowd that had become a mob.

He scaled up over a fence and flattened into a handy alcove while the pursuit pounded past. For a long moment he had not thought he would make his rendezvous with Spock and the landing party. Dr. McCoy's elegant semisurgical makeup jobs on the horn implants were supposed to make Helvan safe for Kirk's democracy. They had not.

He wore the short horns of a Helvan male in a dormant phase, not the deadly spiked horns of a Helvan male in *falat*. The fact that the short horns would strike any Human as devilish was neither here nor there—let alone how they looked on Spock, who had the ears for it. . . .

The Helvan sky shaded from lavender to great flaming clouds of red-gold, which seemed always caught by some sunrise or sunset of the double sun. The Helvan culture was little beyond Stone Age, but much of the city was built of great crystal sheets and columns from some natural quarry. The effect was mirrored red-gold splendor, as easily a scene out of tomorrow as a vision of hell.

Kirk reached to use his communicator. Somehow in this atmosphere of revolution the Helvans had spotted him for a danger. Worse, what was now happening to Spock, Bones, and the landing party?

It suddenly occurred to him to wonder why he had ever divided his forces in this dangerous situation. Then he looked up—and his stomach knotted.

Spock waited for the rendezvous with almost Human impatience. He did not say *worry*. Yet his brief question to Kirk as to the wisdom of separate missions in the street-mob Helvan atmosphere of impending revolution had been brushed aside with uncharacteristic brusqueness. True, time was limited. The disappearances on many planets, including especially this one, were increasing alarmingly.

Once Spock might have pressed the argument further. The 2.8 years he had spent with the Vulcan Masters, attempting to expunge his Human half, had not wholly been erased by his return to the *Enterprise*.

Nonetheless, Spock should have insisted on the foolhardiness of separation.

Kirk was 4.5 minutes late. McCoy was overdue. Chekov appeared to be in some rather vague state. Uhura was missing. And Spock was far from the total logic of Kolinahr. . . .

Kirk backed against the wall. The beings who had come out of nowhere were not Helvan. They were not of any known species.

And they struck Admiral, Acting Captain, James T. Kirk, possibly the most experienced commander in the galaxy in dealing with unknowns, as gut-level terrifying.

They were not large—perhaps a head shorter than he was. They had conical noses on mouthless heads that had a vaguely mechanical look. Yet he sensed that they were beings, not robots. How he knew it, he did not know. But he knew also that there was some sense of utter callousness about them, as if they had no empathy or fellowfeeling for a living being.

He shook off terror and tried a standard nonverbal greeting.

One no-mouth raised an appendage and sent a shimmer like heatwaves toward him.

It seared his nerves. He didn't fall, but he couldn't move. They came to him and one inspected him. Hard finger-tentacles probed into his ears, mouth, then felt him over like prime beef or breeding stock, adding rage and disgust to his terror.

Somehow he sensed that this was all familiar, as if he had even seen pictures of these . . . things.

He knew that the disappearances he had been sent to investigate had come to investigate him.

Ninety-nine out of a hundred who disappeared did not return. And those who did . . .

Spock!

Kirk knew that he had called Spock mentally only after he had done it. Spock was a touch telepath. But Kirk had reached him mentally once or twice—the last time over the light-years from Earth to Vulcan, to haul Spock out of his self-imposed Vulcan exile.*

One of the mouthless things touched Kirk's forehead and the world exploded.

Dr. McCoy bolted forward and caught Spock as the Vulcan suddenly sagged. Uhura caught his tricorder as it fell. They had arrived from separate directions only a moment before the Vulcan's eyes went blank. Chekov came to help take Spock's weight as McCoy went for his medical scanner.

But the Vulcan straightened away from both of them. "That will not be necessary, Doctor. I am undamaged."

"The hell you say," McCoy muttered, running the scanner anyway. "What do you call *that* performance?"

"It was Jim," Spock said. "A distress call. Then . . . nothing."

The Vulcan's eyes narrowed against pain. "Doctor, the Captain may be dead."

"*May* be!" McCoy said. Perhaps only McCoy knew the full truth of times when he and Spock had believed Kirk to be dead. "Then . . . he may *not* be?"

Spock was already consulting his tricorder. "Doctor, I get . . . no sense of his continued existence." He looked

* *Star Trek—The Motion Picture, A Novel,* by Gene Roddenberry

13

up. "And no identi-loc reading. If he were injured, the Helvans would possibly take him to the Helvan hospital you inspected today, Doctor. How bad was it?"

McCoy stared at him. "Hospital? I inspected no hospital."

Chekov and Uhura looked at him strangely. "Doctor," Uhura said, "we *saw* you go into the hospital."

Suddenly something swept through McCoy, a strange feeling of horror and disgust, nameless and terrifying. Abruptly he began to be aware of physical symptoms, pain.

He checked his chronometer. It was much later than he had thought.

"Mr. Chekov," McCoy said, "what happened on your weapons inspection of the Helvan Summer Palace?"

He saw the blank look he knew had been on his own face come to Chekov, then to the beautiful dark features of Uhura as she tried to place her afternoon.

"Memory lapses," McCoy said. "We all have them."

"Fascinating," the Vulcan said. "Possibly even illuminating. I calculate we have moments only before major street violence erupts. We must find the Captain."

He strode off with Vulcan swiftness and the Humans struggled after him.

Chapter Two

McCoy caught Spock's arm and called a halt, indicating he, Chekov, and Uhura were only Human. The Vulcan had set a killing pace, dodging threatening crowds. They had searched everything within reason and some things without.

Spock gave McCoy and the others a moment to breathe, then indicated the forbidding Helvan hospital entrance, some of the dying on its steps. They would have to search there—probably for Jim's body.

"Spock," McCoy said, "even if I don't remember it, that hospital has to be a charnel house. It's the Dark Ages here—when you went to a hospital to *die*."

Spock nodded grimly. "At least, it *was*. Those reports of accelerated change we came here to check indicated a jump of two levels on the Richter scale of cultural development—a matter of centuries, within two years. Let us hope they have had their Pasteur."

He started across the street, but at that moment a commotion erupted out of the alley beside the hospital. An angry mob burst out, manhandling some unseen figure at its center.

Spock and McCoy jolted forward on a surmise—and then they could see that the tousled, battered figure was

Kirk. They could not see whether he was dead or alive. Somehow he had lost his horns. The crowd was ugly, armed, lethal, carrying clubs, knives, swords, and the new powder-and-shot tubes—and the limp body of a starship Captain.

Helvan voices in the crowd were screaming, "Demon! Hornless monster! Burn it!"

McCoy saw Spock plow into the ugly crowd with that Vulcan strength which he seldom fully unleashed, now flinging Helvans aside like tenpins. McCoy, Chekov, and Uhura formed a flying wedge behind him.

McCoy never knew how they got through the knives and clubs. He saw Spock knocking weapons out of hands with a possessed ferocity that would not be blocked. And he found himself and the others wading in with something of the same feeling and with every unarmed combat skill they could muster. Then they reached Kirk.

Spock took Kirk's body up into one arm and turned to cut a path back out of the crowd.

Spock would try for a place where they could not be seen to transport up, not to disturb this culture or chance violating the Prime Directives of noninterference by showing the transporter process.

McCoy saw that they wouldn't make it. Some Helvans were raising the powder-and-shot tubes.

They gained a slight space in the crowd and Spock spoke into his communicator. "*Enterprise*, emergency beam up, now!"

A shot rang past them. Then McCoy sensed the beginning of the transporter effect, which he hated and had never been happier to sense. It could beam his molecules all over the galaxy any time—out of *this*.

McCoy had Kirk on the new translucent main diagnostic table in the *Enterprise* Sick Bay. Dr. Christine Chapel had threatened to have McCoy packed off for treatment, too, and he was realizing that he had picked up a nasty assortment of bruises and a bad cut on one leg. But a temporary spray dressing had to do.

Kirk was the casualty—and of a peculiar kind. The Helvan horns had been removed by some sophisticated process that did not leave wounds. It was, if anything, more sophisticated than the Federation process McCoy or

16

Chapel would have used. Accelerated development or not, it could not possibly be within reach of the native Helvans.

Beyond that, Kirk seemed to have been gone over thoroughly with some sophisticated but extremely callous kind of physical examination.

There were marks of instruments and red marks that seemed to be burns of some unknown kind of radiation.

Kirk was in deep shock, his vital signs critically low.

Spock had stayed in Sick Bay, making his report from there, until moments ago when he had been summoned to the bridge by an urgent eyes-only Starfleet Command communiqué.

Now he came back in, looking grim.

"He'll make it, Spock," McCoy said quickly. "He's responding to the medication for shock."

Spock did not answer, but McCoy saw the lines of the Vulcan's face alter.

It was here in Sick Bay that Spock had come back from deep shock after his mind-link with Vejur, and in that unguarded moment he had taken Kirk's hand, suddenly grasping through that "simple feeling" the sterility of Vejur's vast and terrible logic—and the sterility of Spock's own attempt at the total nonemotion of Kolinahr.

Yet the Vulcan who had sought Kolinahr as an antidote to his pain still remained, maintaining long meditations, silences—stiff with the disciplines of the desert and the cause they had not cured. Whatever cause had sent Spock away from Kirk, McCoy, and the *Enterprise* . . .

This stranger who had come back to them was still not their old Spock, who could usually be teased, deviled, baited—and give as good as he got in his own Vulcan way.

Even with Kirk—maybe especially with Kirk—there had been a certain stiffness.

But now Spock reached out without a word and put his hand on Kirk's shoulder. "Jim!"

Kirk's eyes opened, found Spock's face, then were jolted by some inner horror. His body jerked bolt upright and Spock had to restrain him.

"*Things*—" Kirk seemed to choke and his eyes went blank.

"Tell me what you remember," McCoy said, holding him from the other side.

17

Kirk's eyes focused. "Nothing, Bones. A crowd chased me. I got away. Then—nothing."

"You were late for rendezvous?" Spock asked.

"Yes."

"Then it was at that time I received . . . your call," Spock said.

"I got through on the communicator?"

"No," Spock said. "Not on the communicator."

Kirk looked to McCoy, puzzled.

"Spock damn near collapsed when something knocked you out," McCoy said. "He said he lost the sense of your existence."

Kirk made no comment. "What else?"

"Memory lapses," McCoy said. "We all had them. Me, Chekov, Uhura. Not Spock as far as I know. We lost time. We had no memory, but a vague, overwhelming feeling of horror and . . . shame."

Kirk grimaced. "I'm with you there, Bones. Why . . . shame?"

McCoy shook his head, shrugged. "Helplessness maybe? Something we feel guilty for? I don't know. But something definitely had *you*, Jim."

"Other than Helvans?"

"Jim, Spock found you just in time to keep Helvans from burning you—as a hornless demon."

Kirk reached up to feel for the shorn-off horns.

"Neater than I could have done it," McCoy said.

Kirk managed the first hint of a smile. "Can't say I'll miss them. However, on Mr. Spock . . ."

Spock mustered a trace of the old long-suffering look, but it was forced. "It does require a certain . . . presence . . . to carry them off. The doctor—" He looked at McCoy's head and shook his own, despairing.

Privately McCoy agreed. "I thought they looked rather rakish," he said. "You should see how the women look at Spock now."

Kirk grinned. "Everyone on this ship always sees how the women look at Spock."

McCoy seized the relaxed moment. "That's better. Rest now, Jim."

But Kirk sobered, shook his head. "Something was wrong with us, Bones. Even before the memory lapses. This crew has been together a long time. We track each other, keep each other on the track. Not today. I made a stupid command error—splitting up, letting them pick us off one by one. Nobody stopped me. My apologies, Spock. You tried."

Spock nodded grimly. "Insufficiently."

"Jim," McCoy said, "we *were* apart for nearly three years. You. Spock, me, the others—maybe we lost some of that old edge."

Kirk's eyes considered it. McCoy knew there had been a time when Kirk had wondered whether he had lost his own edge in those years when he had tried to survive the loss of the ship and of all of what he had had out here— in a desk job at the Admiralty.

"No," Kirk said finally. "I could buy that if we hadn't functioned well against Vejur, and since. We have our stresses. But this command crew is still unique—the best in the fleet." He shook his head. "No, it was something down *there*. Mr. Spock, if we could break my memory block, we might have the key to the whole mystery. Would you attempt the Vulcan mind-meld?"

Spock's face became unreadable and he did not immediately answer. The pain he had gone through Kolinahr to try to escape would perhaps become unendurable in the lowering of personal barriers that such a mind-link would involve.

There had been no duty-occasion for a mind-link between these two since Spock had made his decision to go to Vulcan. Until now Kirk had seemed to follow McCoy's advice not to look a gift Vulcan in the ears. But the blunt fact was that, but for the grace of catastrophe, the three years they had been apart might have been forever.

They had dealt with it by falling back on naval tradition and the slow, invisible reweaving of old patterns. Kirk had respected the Vulcan's new, severely posted private space. Now he had to ask.

McCoy stepped into the breach. "Absolutely not," he answered before Spock's silence could become longer. "You are barely out of shock, Jim. We have no idea what kind of blocks, barriers, compulsions, or terrors may have been planted in your mind. Touching them with the mind-meld could throw you right back into terminal shock."

He turned to Spock. "Out, Spock. Doctor's orders. I'm

going to put him to bed. He won't settle down until you leave."

"Sound medical advice," Spock said. "I concur."

"Well, *that's* a first!" McCoy said, but it sounded a little tired even to his ears.

There had been a time when Kirk wouldn't have asked, nor needed to.

Spock turned at the door. "Captain, I was obliged to file a full report. Starfleet Command has ordered us to rendezvous with a fast Federation Scout. Estimated time, fifteen point four hours."

"For what purpose?"

"To take aboard a passenger who will carry sealed orders for us."

"Who?" McCoy asked.

Spock looked at him from behind his Vulcan mask.

"Undisclosed," he said, and left.

Chapter Three

Kirk awoke, screaming.

He heard himself—a shocking sound—and jolted up, thrashing, trying to escape some nameless dread.

Some terrible strength caught him, held him hard. He fought it with the strength of frenzy and could not move it. Suddenly he knew that strength.

"Spock!"

"Here."

For a long moment Kirk let himself remain motionless, trying to recapture the elusive substance of nightmare. But the night shapes all faded to the metallic taste of terror.

Some half-formed thought lingered, and the words that came to him for it were: *What punishment do you set for me?*

But he was not certain whether it was he who asked, or of whom he asked it, for he had not spoken aloud.

Spock answered, "For what offense?"

Kirk shook his head.

"Whom do you ask?" Spock said.

Whom I have offended. It seemed to be the voice of the nightmare that spoke silently in his mind.

Kirk shook himself and drew back. "Forgive me, Mr. Spock. I did not mean to force what you would obviously prefer not to give. The mind-touch will not be required, nor your presence. Thank you. Good night."

Spock did not move. He started to reach for the position of the mind-touch. "My disciplines are at your disposal. Else I would not have come back from Gol."

Kirk pushed the hand away. "Spock, it is a matter of record that you went to the mountains of Gol to wipe out your Human half, including your mother's people, your friends—even the memory of their names. Including mine. And I went to the Admiralty in a handbasket. Sorry if I called you back and disturbed your pristine purity of Vulcan soul. I would have called us both back from some other hell, if necessary. And we both know I'll have you here on any terms, as the unequaled officer you are, if nothing else. But I didn't have to like that cold, Kolinahr bastard who came back aboard and cut friends to whom he owed his life dead. I saw that bastard again tonight, Spock. I won't ask him again. For anything. Dismissed."

The Vulcan's face set hard. "What would you know of Vulcan soul, or of the cost of what you have disturbed— to *me? I am not Human.*"

"If *I* don't know that, who does?"

"*I.*"

Kirk sobered. "Spock, we have lived with that, too. From the *pon farr* to the spores. You've banged me—or us—around once in a while. So what?"

Spock looked down at him. "The danger of my being Vulcan Admiral as of the mind-link, is to *you.*"

Kirk frowned. "What danger, Spock?"

"Duty has forced a link between us too often, too closely. You reached me from Earth to Vulcan, on Gol. You reached me today."

"Or else I would be dead. Both times."

Spock nodded. "For that reason, I cannot shield against that contact. nor can you. But in your untrained state, further contact between us can make your natural mental shielding unselective—unable to shield you from the thoughts of others nor to prevent you from broadcasting your own thoughts. Apart from anything else. Starship command would become an untenable position for you."

Kirk winced. "And I have just spent three years proving how untenable any other position is for me." Then he came up on an elbow. "Spock, I wasn't in command *today.* I'm

22

carrying some alien mental time bomb. Unless I can break it, I'm not fit to command *now*."

Spock looked down at him and without a word, his face still set in the mold of cold ferocity, put his hands on Kirk's face in the position of the link.

Kirk caught Spock's wrists and tried to break the hold, even though he knew that Spock knew how badly he wanted and needed the link. Kirk still had no right to force the Vulcan into that closeness. But the Vulcan hands did know what he needed, and would not be moved. Kirk felt the touch of the mind-probe, merciless this time and tasting of the hot desert winds and cold nights of Gol. The deliberately cold touch met some almost equally cold resistance of his own.

Then it met the black mass of rage and shame that this day had left in him, and even the Vulcan mind-meld could not penetrate that. The effort exploded into fire and he could feel the Vulcan's attempt to withdraw as Kirk sank down into night.

McCoy stood beside Kirk in the transporter room. Both of them looked more presentable than anyone had the right to expect, but Kirk looked as if he had slept in hell.

McCoy had also had a rotten night. It would have been better if he hadn't let Spock relieve him from the night watch over Kirk. But the Vulcan could go without sleep without trouble and McCoy couldn't. Finally McCoy had yielded to that logic.

This morning McCoy learned that Uhura and Chekov, whom he had had under watch in Sick Bay, had also suffered severe nightmares.

Alpha hypnosis and all the standard techniques had failed utterly to break the block in anyone's memory, and Kirk confessed that the Vulcan mind-link had also been tried—and had failed.

Now they were beaming aboard some mysterious hot-shot sent by Starfleet Command whose name was not announced, but who carried sealed orders for their ship. Hell of a way to start a day.

Transporter Chief Rand worked the controls and Kirk, Spock, and McCoy moved on into the chamber.

The image started to form—a massive, solid male, the ears . . . pointed. For a moment McCoy thought that it was Spock's father, Ambassador Sarek of Vulcan. Then the transporter shimmer coalesced into an equally powerful but strange Vulcan who resembled Sarek a little—perhaps mainly in the look of unalterable certainty.

Spock had already raised the paired-fingers Vulcan greeting sign. and McCoy struggled to do the same.

"Live long and prosper." Spock said.

This Vulcan. like Sarek, also looked somewhere on the high side of a hundred, which was Vulcan prime—less than half the Vulcan 250-year life span.

This one looked Human forty and would have a hundred years of Vulcan accelerated thought processes and full adulthood behind him.

"Prosper in command, Spock," the Vulcan said.

Spock stiffened. "Allow me to present Admiral, Acting Captain, Kirk, in command."

The Vulcan glanced at Kirk, then virtually ignored him. "No. I express condolence."

"For *what*, sir?" Kirk demanded, his natural respect for Vulcans sounding strained.

The Vulcan stepped down and moved past Kirk, extending a message cube to Spock. "Kirk is relieved of command."

Kirk stepped to confront the Vulcan. "By what authority?" he asked. "Who *are* you?"

The Vulcan did not answer. Spock said, "Savaj of Vulcan."

It was one of those names people put on lists of ten from all of history they would want to meet in heaven or hell. McCoy had vaguely thought that this particular Vulcan legend had moved on to some Vulcan equivalent.

Kirk stepped back fractionally. "Sir, that is a name I would put beside Commanding Admiral Heihachiro Nogura. I cannot believe that he, or you, would relieve me without showing cause. Are you, personally, relieving me?"

"No." Savaj turned to Spock. "You will assume command of the *Enterprise*."

Spock looked at him stonily. "I resist that order, *S'haile* Savaj."

"Rule of Seven, Spock."

"No proof exists."

"None is required."

Spock's face set.

"Translate, Mr. Spock," Kirk said.

"The closest Starfleet regulation would be, 'Commander possibly unfit to command through no fault of own.' It is nonpunitive, not considered a blot on your record. It requires no proof or hearing. You may request one. To do so would mean leaving the ship."

"My scoutship is waiting should that be your decision," Savaj said. "You are granted the option of remaining aboard in nonpunitive suspension as First Officer."

"I will appeal to Commanding Admiral Nogura," Kirk said.

Savaj shook his head. "It was *he* who granted you the option."

"*You* would not?" Kirk asked.

"Captain, your record is one of excessive risk-taking and dependence on favorable random factors—frequently in the person of your Vulcan First Officer. It is no secret to you that I have more than once opposed in Federation and Starfleet councils decisions that ultimately went in your favor."

"I am aware of that, sir," Kirk said stiffly. "I *had* hoped for a time when we could discuss it in person. Perhaps we could—"

McCoy could see Kirk beginning to turn on the charm-them-out-of-their-tree routine, which he had been known to try even on T'Pau of Vulcan.

"That is useless," Savaj said. "There is no question of fact or logic. I have been apprised of your considerable powers of persuasion, by T'Pau of Vulcan among others."

Kirk looked uncomfortable. McCoy settled for trying to look inconspicuous. Faking Kirk's death with his trusty spray-hypo had been one of McCoy's finest hours—if you didn't try to look at it from the Vulcan viewpoint. T'Pau had not been pleased.

Savaj caught McCoy's discomfiture and glanced at him. "As I have also heard of your penchant for trickery, Doctor. You Humans are an interesting species. One shudders to contemplate an effect that would augment your species' natural weaknesses." He turned to Kirk. "That appears to be the result of the alien effect you have encountered on Helva. Your excessive risk-taking yesterday, for example, Captain. It is in your nature, but you normally try to control that weakness. Yesterday you

25

could not. Your command judgment may now be affected in ways you cannot know. In command you could be deadly. Even Spock could not counterbalance your judgment on Helva."

Kirk faced Savaj bluntly now. "I have considered that possibility, sir. This ship has dealt before with situations in which my command judgment might have been, or was, affected. We have done so without outside help or interference and without relieving me of command. We can do so again."

Spock nodded. "I concur with the Captain. The balance judgment I can offer he has in any case, as if it were his own."

"Commendable," Savaj said, "but insufficient. Command is not by committee. Nor is it properly by a lesser over a superior mind."

"Now wait a minute," McCoy cut in. "Starfleet recognizes special talents, including Vulcan ones. Nowhere does it recognize one species as inferior or unfit to command another. Individual—"

"Have you observed Mr. Spock's individual mind to be superior, Doctor?"

"Superior to *what?*" McCoy protested. "Can Spock calculate to seventeen decimals? Certainly. But as for—"

"That will be enough, Doctor," Savaj said. "Mr. Spock, there is some indication that Vulcans of advanced training may be immune to the alien effect you encountered on Helva. Humans, by their own account, are not immune. Are you, in this instance, Vulcan, Mr. Spock?"

"You are aware of the Vulcan path I have chosen, *S'haile* Savaj."

Savaj turned to Kirk. "I have consented to Nogura's recommendation that you remain aboard, on one ground. Nogura considers that this command crew has a special rapport that is unequaled in Starfleet. There is some evidence that your command-crew rapport may be the only known detector of the alien effect you encountered."

"How?" Kirk asked.

"The rapport made you uniquely aware of each other —Spock detected your disappearance, you noticed each other's memory lapses and unusual behavior. It is believed other starship crews have been affected—and have not known it."

McCoy spoke up. "Are you saying other starships may be commanded by captains who *still* don't know it?"

"Precisely," Savaj said.

"Then they're a damn sight worse off than Jim is," McCoy said. "I'm certifying him medically fit for command."

"Unfortunately, Doctor, your medical judgment is also in question."

"Not on *this* ship," Kirk said. "At need Dr. McCoy will be backed up by his staff and I by mine. Mr. Spock has resisted the suggestion that he take command. What is your position in that event, sir?"

Savaj faced Kirk bluntly. "I am the man who will take command if Spock does not.'"

Chapter Four

Kirk faced Savaj silently for a long moment. "I was not aware that you retained active Starfleet Command rank, Admiral Savaj."

"Life rank," Savaj said. "It serves."

"And if Spock takes command?"

"My recent scientific interests include factors bearing on your mission to investigate accelerated social change on various worlds and associated mysterious disappearances. The *Enterprise* is now ordered to use your special command-crew rapport to track the alien effect. Should that mission fail, Admiral Kirk, my figures indicate that Starfleet will not survive. Nor will galactic civilization."

Kirk found himself struggling to put that in proper perspective. Not long ago he had broken every rule in the book to relieve young Captain Will Decker from command of the *Enterprise*. He, himself, was the better man for the job, Kirk had argued.

"Mr. Spock," Savaj added, "is half Human. I have no such difficulty. It is not clear what effect Spock's mixed heritage may have—nor his well-known rapport with his Captain. I am here, among other things, to observe that particular rapport. It would be of no use to relieve you,

Kirk, if your friendship still makes it command by rapport."

There had been a time when Kirk would have been certain of that. With the strange Spock who had returned from Vulcan, he was not so sure. He turned to lock eyes with Spock, but the Vulcan's eyes were opaque, telling him nothing.

"Spock commands or he does not," Savaj said. "Choose."

Inconceivable to be on this ship and not to command. . . . Not as inconceivable as to let her go off without him.

"Take her," Kirk said to Spock.

Spock looked for a moment at the alternative: Savaj.

"You will log my protest, *S'haile* Savaj," Spock said. "I assume command."

Savaj inclined his head fractionally. "Captain Spock."

Savaj turned toward the door and gathered Kirk up with the gesture of "after you."

"Mr. Kirk," he said.

Kirk overhauled Spock in a corridor. Kirk had escorted Savaj to VIP guest quarters, assigned McCoy to see to the full Vulcan's research needs.

"All right, Spock. Who *is* Savaj—apart from the obvious?"

"Is not the obvious sufficient?"

"It is legend," Kirk said. "Even strictly as a Starfleet Admiral, Savaj set the mold. He is one of my own heroes. But his Starfleet career can't have been more than half his life—even counting basic discoveries in a dozen-odd sciences. Apart from some admiralty decisions early in our last five-year mission, I don't think he's been heard from for years."

Spock made no comment.

"Spock," Kirk protested, "you don't hide a mind like that for ten years. What do you know of Savaj personally?"

Spock stopped by a turbolift. "The *S'haile* Savaj's public life is a matter of record. His privacy is his own."

Kirk turned, shocked. The Vulcan was a blank wall. Kirk made another attempt. "What does *S'haile* mean?"

"A title connoting respect. Its further meaning is also private."

Kirk felt his jaw set. "Spock, this is *us*. Or do you want me to address you as Captain?"

Spock turned to him. "Yes, Mr. Kirk, I do."

He stepped onto the turbolift. Kirk followed, seething.

Spock took the bridge. He moved without ceremony to the center seat. Eyes followed him—the word had preceded him. He took no notice.

"Sir?" Uhura said, perhaps carefully not giving him a title. "Permission for long-range scoutship to depart?"

"Granted," Spock said. "Set course to return to Helvan."

Kirk sat down at the science station. It was, of course, the first station he had fully rated on following the Vejur crisis. The nerve center of the ship, with its override ties to all library computers and ship's functions, it was the first station the Captain had to know, as it was his job to know all of them. This one he would never play like Spock, but he would do in a pinch.

He had not contemplated this particular pinch.

McCoy came onto the bridge, bounced on his heels, barely restraining a harumph for Spock's attention.

Kirk had already keyed the library computer. "Savaj of Vulcan," he read out. "Appointed Starfleet Admiral upon Vulcan entry into Federation. Previous Vulcan background unknown, protected by Vulcan privacy. It is assumed his previous record was commensurate with recommended rank and later exploits. Became Fleet-Commander of all-Vulcan wing of Starfleet with primary responsibility for Vulcan exploration ships, which opened some 32 percent of the now explored galaxy. In his own right Savaj is a scientist of galactic renown in half a dozen fields. Medical discoveries credited with saving of millions of lives. Has taught at Starfleet Academy, Vulcan, and, more rarely, Earth, where cadets called him 'Ironpants'—not to his face." Kirk looked up, summarizing. "Scientific honors —every top award. Starfleet citations and medals, similarly. However—the last ten years of his record are essentially blank."

"On wacation?" Chekov offered from weapons control.

"Vulcans, I am reliably informed, don't *take* vacations,"

Kirk said. Whatever they did, it was certainly no vacation —and no picnic. "Certainly not for ten years," he added.

"Then what *has* he been doing?" Uhura said. "Sir, do you know that this same Savaj wrote the book on alien communications—first lingua code development, much of the basis for the universal translator--the seminal work in my field. There's no way that *that* mind hid under a bushel for ten years. More important, what is he really doing *here?*"

"I can tell you *that*," McCoy said, breaking a sulking silence. "He's driving our celebrated crew up the bulkheads. Gives them that bland, unblinking Vulcan scrutiny —right away they feel they've been running a sloppy ship. He carries himself as if he's Admiral of the Fleet and six kinds of royalty."

Spock looked up for the first time. "That is approximately correct, Doctor, by Vulcan standards."

"Spock, you're always pulling Vulcan royalty out of a hat. I suspect you of being Vulcan royalty yourself. And I don't much care if Savaj *is*. I'm beginning to feel like a witch doctor myself."

Spock brightened. "Indeed, Doctor."

"Have a heart, Spock. Get him off my back."

The turbolift opened to deposit Savaj.

"Doctor," Spock said, "I am aware of no research which indicates that unblinking scrutiny is detrimental to the practice of medicine—or witchcraft."

McCoy groaned. "If you're going to go double-Vulcan on us, Mr. Spock, you'll have to excuse me. I have to go boil a potion—with a slow burn." He turned to leave. "Medical check, Jim. Five minutes."

"There will be some delay, Doctor." Savaj said. "Mr. Kirk. I have run the doctor's medical records on landing party symptoms. You will now run correlation checks, periods of rapid cultural change with records of unusual disappearances. Those who disappear and return may have severe amnesia accompanied by feelings of rage and shame, often with physical symptoms and marks of unusual examination."

Kirk looked up at him. "I have been running those checks, Admiral. Answers are coming now."

The computer began to print out.

CORRELATION: DISAPPEARANCES WITH SUCH
SYMPTOMS KNOWN ON MANY WORLDS. E.G.,
EARTH: TWENTIETH CENTURY. CONTEMPO-
RARY ACCOUNTS BY ALLEGED "CONTACTEES"
UNDER HYPNOSIS SUGGESTED LINK WITH
WIDESPREAD "UFO" PHENOMENON.
   VULCAN: DISAPPEARANCES . . .

Savaj reached down and cut off the printout.

He dropped a recording-cube in the slot and a hologram appeared in the main display tank. "Planets believed affected by the phenomenon we are tracking," Savaj said. They winked on in light in a familiar star map. They included virtually every Federation planet—and a similar spread in Klingon and Romulan Empires, other areas.

Savaj keyed another display. "This is a familiar asymptotic curve, representing a mathematical function that increases geometrically toward infinity. It is well known that if in your twentieth century you had graphed rate of increase of speed of manned travel, it would have remained flat for centuries, then shot up within decades, and within some years after that suddenly approached infinity—at just about the time the speed of light was, in fact, broken. An accomplishment which was then considered impossible."

He flashed another display—now it showed such an asymptotic curve in three dimensions—a composite of curves that all shot up suddenly to infinity.

"Rapid change," Savaj said, "accompanied by outbreaks of savage violence, upheaval, death, and disappearance. This graphs the recent curve on many worlds."

Uhura stared at the display and suddenly leaned forward. "But if all those curves increase to infinity, it would be the end of galactic civilization."

Savaj nodded, indicated one curve. "This projects the death rate."

Spock looked at the graph and projected it. "Soon to exceed the population of the known galaxy."

They looked at each other and began for the first time to grasp the magnitude of the menace. Their mission against Vejur had saved the planet Earth. Now the threat of annihilation included Klingons, Romulans—not only

Chapter Five

Kirk checked into McCoy's office and found the doctor preparing suitable potions: two Saurian brandies.

"I'm not sure the two of us, drunk, can handle a sober Vulcan, let alone two, Bones. Otherwise, it's a hell of a good idea."

"It's prescribed. What's got into Spock?"

"He's 'not Human!' "

"What else is new? Or—did I miss something?"

"*I* must have." Kirk waved it off. "Anything for a headache?"

"Not one that size." McCoy eyed him, seeing bruises that seemed to have showed up since yesterday. "Jim, are you all right?"

Kirk grimaced. "No, I'm not."

McCoy came around the desk. "My God—if you're *admitting* it . . . !"

Kirk waved him off. "Bones, we have to break my mental block. Spock can't help me. There's no mistake about Savaj's figures. This thing has been going on for hundreds of years, maybe thousands, but it's coming to a head *now*. We're drinking to the late, great galaxy."

He handed McCoy a computer printout. It was an account of a disappearance that might have been Kirk's own, down to the rage. shame, marks on the body. Date-line Earth, twentieth century

"Could be a dozen things Jim Hysteria. Wishful think-ing. We know that Earth had some early galactic traffic, but we've never really solved the UFO mystery. There's no hard evidence for the 'contactee' type of report."

"Bones, what hard evidence do we have for what hap-pened to me—and you—yesterday?"

McCoy took the untouched brandy glass out of Kirk's hand. "I can recommend the neopentothal."

"Make it a double."

McCoy administered the hypnotic drug, fine-tuned the sensitive scan that should help break down virtually any unconscious block, patient willing

He began to ask the preliminary relaxing questions—name. rank. After a moment's hesitation Kirk answered with some satisfaction. "Captain James T. Kirk, Com-mander, U.S.S. *Enterprise*" Then he frowned as if there were something more he should have remembered, but dismissed it. That was who he was. That was who he had always wanted to be.

McCoy pressed on. The hypnoscan showed areas that Kirk defended strongly as a matter of privacy, and with the uncommon dynamic quality of Kirk's mind, which Spock had long ago sensed in the mind-link. McCoy knew what some of those private areas were. could wish he knew more about one or two, but he would not have probed.

He was looking for the main mass of resistance that would be the recent trauma And there it was, like some large, gray, foreboding presence Of dangerous size.

"You are moving back in time," McCoy murmured, "back through the night."

Kirk's head started to lash back and forth in negation. "*Past* the night," McCoy said hastily. "It is yesterday afternoon. Everything is all right The crowd's rough, but you're on your way to the rendezvous . . ."

Kirk relaxed to wary intentness. His body was stilled with the body's natural release of the biochemical that kept the muscles from moving violently in dreams. But McCoy could see in the trace movements, like a puppy's dream of being chased, the gathering of anger in the crowd, the start of the chase. "Crowd . . . closing on me . . ."

McCoy could follow the chase on Kirk's face—only the ordinary fear and coping with it of an experienced man, none of the gut-terror of trauma. Then there was a moment when Kirk got past the danger, thought himself safe . . .

Then—terror struck. McCoy had never seen that kind of fear on Kirk's face. He saw Kirk try to fight it down, respond, make contact. "Things . . ." he murmured. "No mouths. No . . . fellow-feeling . . ." Then he seemed to freeze. "Don't touch me . . . Stop . . . *Spock!*"

Suddenly the terror burst through the hypnotic state, even defeating the body's own drug against movement. Kirk came up off the platform like a mad thing—a crazed animal pushed beyond the limits of Human terror. He flung McCoy against a wall without noticing it and crashed blindly across Sick Bay, smashing into things. McCoy struggled to stay conscious, to get to an alarm . . .

Before McCoy could reach an intercom the doors burst open and Spock was there, catching the blind, animal Kirk, stopping the frantic movements, holding him by main force.

McCoy saw Savaj move in from the doorway, the full Vulcan's face unyielding, emotionless, his Vulcan strength ready to assist. But Spock required no assistance.

McCoy moved in with a counterhypnotic hypo, but before he could reach Kirk Spock's presence communicated itself directly. Kirk stopped, stayed still, seemed to collect himself, then focused his eyes.

Spock turned Kirk around and inspected him for a moment, saw sanity, and let his own features harden to coldness. "Mr. Kirk, what is the meaning of conducting a hazardous medical experiment involving key personnel of this ship without consulting its commander?"

"Consulting!" Kirk flared. "Who appointed *you* God?" He caught himself, mastered the outburst a little, saw Savaj looking on with infuriating coolness. Kirk smiled dangerously. "Forgive me." He inclined his head fractionally in Savaj's direction. "I had forgotten who had that authority." He moved away from Spock and met his eyes. "Captain Spock, apart from anything else, I am now First Officer and Science Officer here. It is within my authority

37

to conduct research. and within McCoy's prerogatives to do what he considers necessary as Chief Medical Officer."

Spock shook his head "Not anymore. Circumstances render both your judgment suspect Mr. Kirk, your normal tendency to risk yourself sometimes in unwarranted manners, may be magnified by the same effect that you admit affected your judgment yesterday. It has done so again. At minimum you should have requested my presence as a protection against what just happened."

Kirk grimaced, caught by his own sense of fairness. "I apologize for that. To you too Bones."

McCoy shrugged "I've never known anybody to break out of a hypnoscan like that Jim. What they did to you must have been—intolerable Being Spock. He definitely contacted some kind of beings. 'Things,' 'no mouths,' no 'fellow-feeling,' he said."

Spock nodded, as if it came as no great surprise. "How did you know to come charging in here, Spock?" McCoy asked.

"It is my responsibility to know Doctor." If Savaj noted that that was not an answer he gave no sign.

Spock turned to Kirk "Mr Kirk I did not seek command, but if I command I command. A ship does not serve two masters. You will respect that or confine yourself to quarters."

Kirk looked at him stubbornly for a long moment and McCoy thought that there was an anger there that would not soon subside They had been through too much together for Spock to take his tone with him—and in front of Savaj. Kirk's own command over Spock had been definite, but almost always with a light hand.

But how many times must Spock have wished that he could order Kirk not to pull some particularly dangerous stunt?

And now he could.

Even their resident Vulcan must be just Human enough to relish that.

Finally Kirk nodded "Understood . . . *sir.*"

Spock inclined his head in acknowledgment. "If you are fit, you may continue with Admiral Savaj's briefing tour of the ship."

Kirk turned on his heel and went out with Savaj.

38

Chapter Six

Kirk walked stiffly with Savaj, more irritated with himself than with Spock—which was saying something. Bad enough that this full Vulcan had seen Kirk panicked and being dressed down in front of him. But also Kirk had lost his own temper.

"Admiral, I apologize for that remark about appointing God."

"My authority does not extend quite that high, Commander."

Kirk looked at Savaj, trying to read Vulcan devilment —or mere literal-mindedness.

"Neither does Spock's," Kirk ventured wryly, "although apparently one could get an argument about that in some quarters."

The Vulcan's face remained impassive—much harder to read than Spock's father Sarek's, doubtless because this full Vulcan had not married Spock's formidable Human mother, Amanda.

Kirk shrugged. "Captain Spock's point about requesting his presence as protection was well taken. I regret you had to see the consequences of that omission."

"One regrets consequences, Commander, not the seeing of them."

Kirk clamped down on his temper again. "Yes. Of course. What would you prefer to see next, Admiral? Engineering?"

"Your recreation deck."

"Rec deck? Certainly Forgive me—I hadn't thought a Vulcan would be much interested." The turbolift arrived and Kirk gave the destination as they stepped in.

"This is predominantly a Human ship. Commander. Maintenance of its most significant mechanisms in operating condition does frequently take place there, does it not?"

"Yes, it does. I've often wondered what would perform that function on an all-Vulcan ship."

Savaj turned to look at him "You would have had substantially more difficulty with that Commander, as a lone Human there than Spock has had here."

They emerged onto the rec deck. The great vaulted space was filled with Humans and a variety of other species who worked almost as hard at their play.

Most of the special-purpose alcoves opening off the walls at all heights were open too—everything from specialty shops to chess alcoves to coffee places and conversation pits, plus privacy alcoves some reached by null-grav shaft. In the physical activity areas even the air was full with null-grav sports The great sea wall opened on the landscaped tank filled with playful swimmers—and the liquid that resembled water, except that air breathers did not drown in it.

Everywhere was talk. laughter, bright bodies flashing with trained grace—the look of a happy ship. Few knew the seriousness of the present problem. and while Kirk caught some curious looks at him his crew seemed to regard any interruption of his command as local and temporary. They had long been accustomed to regarding Spock as a kind of extension of himself. Some nodded and he saw the word *Captain* on their lips.

He turned to Savaj. "Spock finds certain pleasures here. Would a full Vulcan find them . . illogical?"

"Unrestful, perhaps," Savaj said "But then a Vulcan would not attempt to use them for that purpose."

40

"What would I have found difficult as, say, your First Officer, sir?" Kirk asked.

"I assure you, Mr. Kirk, you would have found it quite impossible."

"Specify?"

"To push the buttons. To calculate what a Vulcan would do in infant school. To avoid broadcasting emotions to the distraction of all." Savaj saw Kirk getting irritated. "Most of all, to calculate the logic of risk. Under my command you would have failed to do so only once."

"Mr. Spock has attempted to deal with that problem, perhaps with some success. But it remains true that risk is our profession."

"Logical risk."

Kirk smiled. "I know of no logic by which a fish climbs up on land or a man to the stars. But my species does it —and yours, sir."

"And is that how you justify the risk you are taking with Spock?"

Kirk looked at him sharply. "What risk?"

Savaj did not answer immediately. After a moment he said, "By what right do you hold a superior mind under your command while refusing to take his advice on matters of risk—exposing him also to the consequences of your actions?"

"It is a matter of record that Spock has been free to accept his own command for many years now. He has refused to do so."

"Vulcan loyalty to a commander is considered a cardinal virtue."

"So is loyalty, Human or Vulcan, to a friend, Admiral. I take Mr. Spock's advice when I can. When I expose him to risk I know at least that he serves as he chooses."

"He serves as he must." Savaj dismissed it with a hand. "Commander, it is also of record that you play chess. I would find that instructive."

Kirk inclined his head fractionally. "We could play the infant school version, I'm sure."

Savaj merely raised an eyebrow blandly. "That will do."

Kirk had put an edge on it, and he immediately regretted that. It might too easily be true.

If you made a list of the ten best minds in the galaxy,

you could make a case that Savaj was at least two of them. On the other hand, Kirk played chess with Spock.

The moment they started to set up the three-dimensional chessboard it became a shipwide event. Everybody off duty imperceptibly drifted over. One of Uhura's young communications ensigns manned a talkie with which he evidently intended to patch in a running account to the duty stations. They had done that now and then for some particularly historic game between Kirk and Spock. But here was fresh meat. Probably Kirk's.

Kirk saw little flurries of betting and bookmaking in the background and was pleased to see that the odds weren't totally one-sided. Doubtless a mistaken loyalty. He saw Chief Engineer Montgomery Scott, who had been watching over Kirk at every chance since Helvan, making book on him to win.

Kirk heard an ensign murmuring, "Don't worry. The Captain'll psych him out."

"I wouldn't count on it," Yeoman Trian whispered, looking at Savaj, "but I'll root for it."

McCoy got wind of the game and strolled in. He sidled over to Kirk, ran a medical scanner. "Vitals still not up to par, Jim. I'd advise rest."

Kirk flashed a subdued grin at McCoy for giving him a graceful way out, but shook his head. "Unrestful, doubtless, but man does not live by rest alone."

Kirk drew white and played a standard but solid king's pawn opening to a standard reply, and for a few moves they developed their pieces to control key squares, ranks, and levels, feeling each other out, trading an occasional piece evenly or for advantage of position.

Savaj had the advantage of that Vulcan mind, which could calculate alternatives like a multiphase computer. Most Vulcans who played Humans gave them at least a queen handicap—about what a Human would give a bright six-year-old. Kirk had been maybe too stubborn to accept one from Spock and had gotten his pants beaten off, routinely, until at some point he had begun to develop subtle psychological advantages—which sometimes worked.

It had spoiled him for playing most Humans.

Spock came in now, did not speak, but stood watching.

"Pawn to queen's Level One," Kirk said. "Admiral, would you care to define 'logical' risk?"

He half-expected Savaj to insist that full Vulcans did not converse over chess. But Savaj answered, "A child's definition begins with exclusions—no risk that is unnecessary, avoidable, reducible by ordinary or extraordinary means. Example: How would you describe a style of command, Mr. Kirk, in which a commander knows a cloud-creature to be lethal to himself and his kind, harmless to a better qualified First Officer under his command, yet goes to face the creature himself over that officer's strong protest?"*

Kirk gave Savaj points for psyching, too. How was it that the full Vulcan had picked out, from their unfortunately too well known record. the very incident that was Spock's classic example? Kirk looked up to see Spock's face. And did it really rankle so deeply with the Vulcan First Officer still?

"That First Officer," Kirk said, "was right."

Savaj looked up, surprised, as if Kirk might be showing some promise.

Spock managed to keep expression off his face.

"That commander," Kirk said, "may have had certain thoughts, intuitions, even hunches, at the time that suggested that there might be a need for a second live bait, which could only be himself. That proved to be the case. If the cloud-creature had escaped to spawn, the consequences were unthinkable. Nevertheless, the First Officer would have been safe—and might have been quick enough on the first try."

"A 'nevertheless' is not an admission of error, Mr. Kirk," Savaj said.

Kirk moved a rook to line it up, file and level, with his queen.

"No. It is not," he agreed. "Mr. Spock was right, and I was playing a long-shot hunch that I wouldn't have been able to explain properly then or since. That case may have been a mistake, potentially fatal. But I know that I have often gone with the subliminal 'feel' of such decisions— maybe a form of lightning calculation I can't use consciously. Very often they work out."

---

* "Star Trek" episode entitled "Obsession."

"Until the day when the favorable random factors run out."

Kirk met the Vulcan's eyes. "Until that day."

Savaj had answered his move by taking Kirk's rook—and leaving a small opening on a crucial square on king's Level One.

"Logical risks," Savaj said, "must reduce losses to the bearable—or the inescapable."

"And if losses would be intolerable and the odds are absurd?"

"Reevaluate," Savaj said. "Reinforce. Refuse risk. Make peace." He looked at Kirk levelly. "Die, if necessary. The universe does not always arrange the triumph of virtue."

"No, but I prefer to rearrange the universe to that effect when possible. Change the name of the game—"

He looked up at Spock. It was an argument they had had very early, when Kirk had run his Corbomite bluff against the overwhelming force of Balok's great ship. Spock had argued an analogy with chess—in the face of overwhelming force, concede. Kirk had changed the game to poker and bluffed to convince Balok that Kirk held all the cards—in the shape of a self-destruct weapon that would destroy them all.* Spock had never again conceded defeat. He stood now watching, face impassive.

Kirk made his move, through the small opening with the bishop he had reserved for the purpose while distracting with a more visible threat. "Check," he said.

"I *told* you the Captain would psych him!" some exuberant *Enterprise* voice said. "Mate in one move."

Kirk saw it then. A layer-on-layer trap designed precisely to draw him into trying his psychout move, playing on his slightly free-wheeling, risk-taking style.

Savaj had only one move, and it would both block Kirk's check and checkmate his king. It was as neat a trap and as complete a reading of him as Kirk had ever seen.

He reached out and tipped over his king in acknowledgment. "Thank you," he said. "I found it most instructive."

But Savaj was already rising. "Captain Spock, a word with you. Mr. Kirk."

---

* "Star Trek" episode entitled "The Corbomite Maneuver."

He moved off with them across the rec deck, McCoy trailing.

"Captain Spock, you have been his First Officer how long?"

Spock's look became cold. "The figure is a matter of record."

Savaj nodded toward an exercise mat they were approaching. "You also work out with him."

"On occasion," Kirk said He thought he saw where Savaj was going and resented it on Spock's behalf.

"I would like to see such a workout." Savaj said.

Kirk looked at Spock. and Spock shrugged an eyebrow. They went to the changing cubicles.

It was Savaj's turn to raise an eyebrow when they came back in the belted jackets and close-fitting breech clouts of the Vulcan *asumi* discipline.

"A green sash, Mr. Kirk? That is a considerable achievement for a Human."

"Spock is a considerable teacher."

They crossed right arms to each other's right shoulder, in token of a match not to the death. then released, bowed, paused for one moment of attunement.

The *V'asumi* duo-katas were an exercise and an art form based on a simulation of combat. As such they were fatally fast and potentially lethal—if either partner missed a beat in reading what the other was to do or in demonstrating a blow millimeters short of deadly impact.

Perfectly done, a *V'asumi* became almost a dance of menace, and of perfect control—the ancient dance of sworn warrior brothers.

They had given no name to it when they had learned it, and they had not done it since Spock returned from Vulcan. But by unspoken consent it was what they would do in the face of Savaj.

The entire off-duty crew assembled again to watch.

They dissolved into action.

Kirk feinted and attacked. Spock read him and slipped him over his shoulder. throwing him by his own momentum. But Kirk used the same momentum and a leg scissors to bring the Vulcan down to one knee. Spock slipped Kirk's hold and caught him again Kirk smashed with an elbow—pulling the blow by millimeters. In combat it would have smashed Human ribs into lungs—and possibly

45

inconvenienced a Vulcan. Spock locked Kirk against his chest in a hold that threatened to set in for the winter; somehow he slipped out of it—turned and launched a high kick. Spock caught it out of the air, caught his momentum, and carried him into a high lift. It was a terminal *V'asumi* maneuver. In combat Spock could have done what he wished.

They turned it into a flying dismount, Spock giving him the momentum for a high back flip to a landing in front of Spock. They locked wrists in warrior's acknowledgment and stepped back to bow.

There was spontaneous applause from the crew—rather long and loud. Kirk raised a hand to subdue it and walked with Spock to a stone-faced Savaj.

Savaj indicated with a fractional jerk of his head "Come with me," and they walked through the crowd toward the changing cubicles. McCoy joining them.

"I never thought I'd see that again," McCoy muttered.

Out of earshot of the crew in the changing corridor Savaj turned on Spock. "Call thee this Human friend, Spock? Then by what right soften him to his death? Think you a Romulan would handle him so gently?" The Vulcan formal mode sounded scathing.

Spock faced Savaj and there was some primitive look between them. "He has survived Romulans."

"Thy friend has no brother. His own fire-brother condemns him to the first savage. It is no act of friendship."

"The practice is *V'asumi* not *K'asumi*. The difference in strength is ineradicable."

"*V'asumi* may properly restrain strength, not power. Difference is no excuse for acceptance of less than full potential. Centuries ago the ineradicable difference argument was made against the female of this species."

Spock shrugged. "Early studies showed, in that case, a potential strength increase of sixty percent—later, still more."

"And where is *your* interspecies study, Spock? The Human potential is limited only by acceptance of limits. How can you let this Human—or any Human—go into battle in this condition?"

Spock looked as if he would be embarrassed if he knew how—and he did.

"Mr. Spock has respected our diversity," Kirk began.

Savaj managed an impolite expression. He inclined his head toward a changing booth and stepped into it. Spock punched in a code for the fabricator. Energy shimmered behind the transluscent door and Savaj stepped out momentarily in an *asumi* jacket—tied with the scarlet sash that Spock also wore—the highest rank. But Savaj's had a fine gold chain woven into it.

He turned without a word and Spock followed him back out to the mat.

"Spock," McCoy muttered under his breath, "you don't have to do this."

"Yes, Doctor, I do."

Spock and Savaj squared off on the mat, locked right arms, bowed—and became the sudden, feral incarnation of all Vulcan. The desert lived here, and the *le matya*.

Kirk understood suddenly that the green sash he had earned with such pride was only a Vulcan child's earning, doubtless earned by Vulcans before the Kaswan trial at the age of seven.

Kirk was the child.

These two were the adult.

Kirk could not follow the moves—bone-jarring throws, nerve holds that would have felled an ox—demonstrated only to the point of fading consciousness here, blows that would have shattered bone, now pulled to a dull crunch that would still have filled McCoy's Sick Bay if tried on Humans.

For a moment beyond the fight Kirk caught Uhura's eyes, shocked, and rapt—the look of a jungle huntress. He caught a somewhat similar expression on other faces —Rand's, Trian's.

But he was focused on Spock. Every eye in the crew was riveted to Spock.

For all Kirk had known, he had still never known the Vulcan's full potential. Once Kirk had seen the end of a fight, and an enemy, who had called that Vulcan's full potential forth.* But this was a demonstration of consummate skill that went on long beyond the point where one Vulcan would have killed the other in a fight to the death.

* *The Price of the Phoenix*, by Sondra Marshak and Myrna Culbreath

Kirk caught himself wondering: In a fight to the finish between these two, who would finish?

Savaj was older—in that ageless Vulcan way that only appeared to make him stronger, more massive, full-grown, weathered oak against Spock's more slender strength.

On the other hand, Spock had that strength which did not seem to come from muscle alone, but from somewhere out of the ground—maybe from that indomitable will by which he had come to live, an alien among strangers.

Spock got in a good, hard-slamming fall and looked as if it gave even his Vulcan half some satisfaction. One for captain and friend possibly, or just one for himself.

But "Ironpants" Savaj could take it as well as dish it out. The fall would have put a Human off the duty roster for a week. Savaj was up in one controlled roll, caught Spock, and put him down with a force that seemed to rock the deck.

Spock got up rather slowly and his face wore some trace of the savage look that Kirk had seen on occasion. It did not bode well even for Ironpants Savaj.

"Jim!" McCoy muttered. "Aren't you going to stop this?"

"How, Bones? I'm open to suggestions." In fact, his instinct was to order it. The difficulty with that was that he was not in command. And if he *had* been, it looked a lot like ordering a cessation of hostilities between *Tyrannosauri rex.*

He was considering pulling some stunt . . .

Savaj gave the hand-signal-of-senior that the encounter was ended. Spock's jaw set, but he straightened, bowed, and gave the countersignal.

Then Savaj turned to Kirk, inviting with an eyebrow. There was a faint gasp from somebody as the crew realized what he meant.

Spock signaled Kirk imperceptibly: *No.*

But it was an offer Kirk couldn't refuse. Nor did he really want to. He was none too pleased with the thought of stepping onto the mat with that *le matya* after what he had just seen. On the other hand, even Savaj wouldn't give him the full Vulcan treatment, and he did know a move or two.

He went in with some thought of getting in at least one good lick for what Savaj still had to know about this mission and wasn't telling—and for the way he had just talked to Spock.

Kirk stepped onto the mat. He sized Savaj up as they bowed and decided that that had been a serious mistake.

Then Savaj moved, and he was certain of it.

The full Vulcan put him down in an easy fall, with zero effort at all. Savaj half-cushioned the fall, then gave him a hand up, let him set himself, and make his move—and took him down as easily again.

There was no sense of excessive force or massive use of the great strength. It was merely skill and the simplicity with which adult would restrain child or hulking male some untrained, slender youngster.

Kirk was not untrained, but against this hundred-year skill and depth of power he might as well have been.

He felt something snap and went in with the best move Spock had taught him—to try one fall in earnest. It was supposed to work against superior strength. A flying use of body momentum—

Savaj caught him out of the air, absorbing the momentum without difficulty, and to Kirk's cost—as if a tree caught him. Then Savaj put him down, hard—not full force, but jarring.

For a long moment he pinned Kirk down.

"That's better, Commander. Honest Human emotion. Rage. Would you care to try for the sixty percent? You will need it where we are going."

Kirk strained against him with every muscle he owned. Savaj didn't flicker a muscle, but if full Vulcan eyes could laugh. these did.

Kirk stopped. "I'll have it," he said through his teeth.

Savaj rose in one movement and pulled him to his feet. "Tomorrow, then?"

Kirk nodded. Savaj strode off toward the changing cubicles.

Kirk turned to Spock, jerked his head toward the mat. "You heard the man. Let's go." If it was still the command tone. he was beyond caring.

Spock shrugged fractionally and obeyed. stepped onto the mat. Form did not demand a second ritual. Kirk tried a quick move on Spock. For once Spock answered like a Vulcan, not at full strength, but with more power than he had ever used on Kirk in his right Vulcan mind. He

49

caught a lock hold and Kirk strained against it with all he had, as if he would build the 60 percent on the spot.

But it was not to be that simple. Spock kept the hold until the point was well established, then released him and let him turn to lock eyes.

Kirk knew his own eyes were now making the accusation Savaj had made.

"Tomorrow, Mr. Spock," he said flatly.

"You forget yourself, Mr. Kirk." The tone was Vulcan and the demand in the dark Vulcan eyes was inflexible.

Kirk caught a hold on his temper and lowered his eyes fractionally in acknowledgment. "Captain."

He felt the crew looking on in shock. McCoy was moving in with some idea of breaking up the moment.

Kirk turned and moved off toward the changing cubicles, realizing that he was angrier than he had known, probably more than he had a right to be. Nonetheless, he was.

McCoy followed Spock into the changing corridor, grumbling at him. "Did you have to call him down in front of the whole crew? Rank gone to your head, Spock? Or is it those devil horns you won't let me take off? Acting the part?"

"Do not forget *yourself*, Doctor," Spock said, opening the door of a cubicle.

"*Captain*," McCoy said, not respectfully. "Come off it, Spock. You said for years you didn't want command. Did a Vulcan lie?"

"What I want is irrelevant, Doctor. What I have is command. You will excuse me."

He stepped in and closed the door of the cubicle. McCoy heard the faint sound of programming the fabricators for a change. Colors started to shimmer behind the translucent door.

Then McCoy realized that some sound was subliminally wrong, the pattern of forming fabric also somehow wrong.

He reached for the outside release, but it did not open the door. There was a thrashing inside and a muffled sound. McCoy rammed a shoulder against the door, but bounced off.

Suddenly Savaj was there. He smashed his fist through the tough door, then ripped it out.

Spock was naked, enclosed in some transparent cocoon of thick stuff that seemed to be shrinking rapidly around every part of his body, swiftly crushing in throat and Adam's apple, threatening ribs and internal organs.

Savaj ripped Spock out of the cubicle and tore at the fibrous stuff at face and throat with his hands.

Kirk appeared from somewhere and also started trying to clear the stuff, but it would not yield to Human hands —as McCoy also was finding out.

Savaj ripped it apart at Spock's throat and mouth, cleared an airway, but it was still crushing his whole body. Spock did not cry out, but it was clearly beyond even Vulcan techniques for controlling pain.

Savaj lifted him and bundled him into the next cubicle, closed the door, and programmed the fabricator to strip.

"If *this* one is defective, too—" Kirk began.

But Savaj had hit the control. Colors shimmered behind the panel—life or death. Savaj snapped the lock on the door as they faded. Spock collapsed out into their arms.

McCoy checked him with his hands. Alive. Breathing. Nothing broken that he could find in a moment. The heartbeat ridiculously fast, even for a Vulcan—but McCoy wasn't complaining.

"Bones?" Kirk demanded.

"Okay," McCoy said. "He'll be all right."

Kirk nodded. He had pulled off his *asumi* jacket and was putting it over the naked Spock as the crew began to pour into the corridor. Then he turned to the problem, picked up a scrap of the fibrous stuff Savaj had torn off Spock's throat.

"Mr. Scott. This is thickening fabricator base, isn't it?"

Scott took the scrap. "Aye, Captain."

"Check the cubicle, Engineer."

"Aye, sir." Scott leaned his head in, snapped open a panel. "I'm nae certain how it was done, but something bollixed the programming to transport in straight, hot base instead of a uniform. It would make a deadly shrink-wrap."

Kirk looked down at Spock. "If Spock had been alone—"

"More precisely," Savaj said, "if *I* had not, unexpectedly, been nearby, Captain Spock would be dead. Vulcans

51

are somewhat vulnerable to asphyxiation and to extreme pressure on ears and body. No Human in your crew would have had the strength to aid Spock in time."

Kirk nodded. "Your actions were timely and exemplary, sir, and I thank you."

"One does not thank necessity, Commander. Nor random factors. There was every reason for someone to suppose that I had long ago gone."

"Someone?" Kirk said. "Are you implying that someone *did* this?"

"I imply nothing. Random failure of the cubicle Captain Spock used earlier—to which he would almost certainly return, since he would have left a transporter hold code for personal articles there—seems excessively convenient."

Kirk straightened. "There is no one on my ship, Admiral, who would attempt to kill Mr. Spock."

Savaj met his eyes. *"I* do not know that, Commander. Nor do you. There is at least one stranger aboard your ship."

"You, Admiral?" Kirk almost smiled. "Do you wish me to consider you a suspect?"

"Certainly," Savaj said. "We are faced with what is either an inexplicable accident or a still more inexplicable attempt on Spock's life. We are pursuing a still less explicable alien effect. Nothing is beyond suspicion." He looked at Kirk, now wearing only the loincloth of the *asumi* outfit. "You left the floor some minutes ago, Mr. Kirk. Why had you not changed?"

Kirk looked shocked. *"Me?* Kill *Spock?"* He shook his head helplessly. "Wrong track, Admiral. The fact is"—he looked a little sheepish—"I went to cool off."

"The fact is, you had something from which to 'cool off.' Captain Spock twice used his authority to reprimand you—once in front of me, once before your whole crew."

Kirk dismissed it with a shrug. "Irritating, sir. Scarcely lethal." He turned. "Mr. Scott, take that system apart. Find out what happened. Bones, get Spock to Sick Bay."

"That will not be necessary, Mr. Kirk," Spock said. He lifted his head from McCoy's arms. "I am functional. Clear the corridor. Savaj may remain."

McCoy said, "I'm not moving, Captain Spock."

"That is your prerogative, Doctor. No one else's." He

52

looked at Kirk, and Kirk looked ready to take something apart, thought better of it, turned stiffly, and left.

Savaj punched a robe code and let it form in an empty cubicle, retrieved it, and brought it to Spock. Spock pulled the robe on to replace the skimpy coverage of Kirk's *asumi* jacket.

But the Vulcan was barely into the robe when a red alert sounded.

Chapter Seven

McCoy tried momentarily to restrain Spock, but the Vulcan was up and moving for the intercom at the end of the corridor. They met Kirk there. Kirk had beaten Spock to it by old reflex.

Sulu was already on the small screen. "Helm. Unidentified presence. Vessel of unknown type. Maybe it's *not* a vessel. It seems to pop in and out—like a skipping stone—maybe on a dimensional interface."

Savaj nodded as if with satisfaction. *"That* brought them."

Spock turned on him. "Brought whom?"

"Unknown," Savaj said. "Possibly whoever is studying what we just did."

Spock looked at him narrowly. He turned to the intercom. "On my way. Admiral, Mr. Kirk." Spock handed Kirk the *asumi* jacket he still held, as if urging Kirk to cover himself, and moved for the turbolift. McCoy trailed them.

In the turbolift Spock turned on Savaj. "Admiral, you will be good enough to explain whether or in what manner you are using this ship to draw some alien presence—without the prior knowledge of its commander."

Savaj inclined his head. "Unorthodox, Captain, but essential. The hypothesis I was testing required that you have no prior knowledge."

"Specify."

"I believe that the presence we are studying is studying *us*."

"Scientists?" Kirk said. "Some alien task force?"

"Experimenters," Savaj said. "Source unknown. Purpose unknown."

"Then what did you count on to draw them?" Kirk asked.

"Mr. Kirk, you and I played the most combative and territorial of intellectual games. I baited you and Captain Spock on grounds of your well-known friendship—and with uncomfortable truths. I arranged for three of the most competitive men in the galaxy to meet in its fiercest combat sport. I may even have succeeded beyond my aims if Captain Spock's accident was anything else. But in any case, *they* came."

"Are you saying," Kirk asked, "to study . . . aggression?"

"I believe that is what I *said*."

"Flawlessly logical." Spock said coldly. "Presuming that *is* the experimenters' intent—and that they do not dissect subjects who exhibit the required characteristics."

Savaj's look was glacial. "That is a distinct possibility, Captain Spock. However, we are not necessarily expected to survive this mission. We are merely expected to save the galaxy. If possible."

They reached the bridge.

An alien ship loomed on the screen, maybe twenty times their size.

"Whatever you gentlemen are doing," McCoy complained, "it's *working*."

Kirk watched the alien ship skip-fade out into nothingness. It still showed on the mass scanners, but it reflected all penetration scans and might as well have been a black box. Now an invisible black box.

"Lingua code," Spock ordered, but they all sensed it was useless.

Kirk fought down a sudden recurrence of nausea and shame. He was still shaken by that scene in the corridor when Spock had nearly died. Then something solidified into anger within him, Savaj had been playing with them, pulling the strings of what he knew would get a rise out of them on some deep level. It *had*. Even the chess had been as cutthroat as Kirk had ever played. Savaj had seen to it that he was defeated on all grounds, before his crew, but worse, had implied that Spock had been pulling punches on him.

Not only in *asumi*. In chess.

He tried to shake the anger off, remembering the moment in the corridor when he had been certain that the fibrous stuff had done its work. If Spock had died . . .

He stood up and went over to the command seat. "You shouldn't be here, Captain Spock. There's no immediate action. Let me take it and you go with McCoy."

"Negative. Unnecessary."

Kirk dropped his voice. "Spock, don't play ironman. You were close to death. You could have internal injuries."

"Mr. Kirk, you will not argue my orders."

Kirk flared. "I will if they are 'illogical,' Spock, as you damn well argued mine—and properly. And on that subject, you are now going to work me out at full speed and skill to build maximum strength. And if I catch you in less than full Vulcan mode, in that or in chess, you will rue the day."

He had said it with some heat, but with some touch of the old humor.

But suddenly he saw the primitive look that had flared in Spock's eyes against Savaj. "You do not command," Spock said, "and you will not threaten."

Kirk moved closer—with what intent he was not certain—but there was some red haze behind his eyes.

"Mr. Kirk," Spock snapped, "you will confine yourself to quarters."

Kirk stopped, stunned. Finally he held to some thread of discipline.

"Yes, sir," Kirk said, and turned on his heel and left the bridge.

McCoy signaled and popped into Kirk's quarters almost before hearing the muffled "Come."

"What do you call *that* performance?" McCoy said.

"What do you call *Spock's?*" Kirk waved it off. "Sorry,

Bones. I'm on edge. What happened to Spock down there didn't help. I shouldn't have argued—but I still didn't figure Spock to let command go to his head."

"Why not?" McCoy said. "He must have despaired of you often enough." He came with the scanner. "Actually, you both need your heads examined. Which I will. That's a high stress reading, Jim."

Kirk grimaced, rubbed his temples. "Headache. Bones, for a second on the bridge I had that feeling again—the shame, anger—"

"And blew it off at Spock."

"Yeah." Kirk confessed glumly. He turned to the intercom. "Bridge. Captain Spock, my apologies, and I have something to report about possible alien effect. Permission to return to duty?"

Spock's face on screen was the Vulcan mask.

"Report."

"On the bridge I experienced a repetition of the previous effect, including guilt, anger."

Spock nodded. "Fascinating. Apology noted, Mr. Kirk. Your presence is not required at the moment. Remain in your quarters and follow medical advice to rest."

Kirk started to protest, but the Vulcan had ended the transmission.

"Sound medical advice," McCoy said.

"Get out of here, Bones."

McCoy stood his ground. "You can't treat this lightly, Jim. You've been worked over by aliens who've left some implanted effect tough enough to break you out of a hypnoscan in a blind fury."

Kirk sobered, nodded. "I know it, Bones. But how can I get a grip on that? Is there some other medical test we can try?"

"You didn't get into enough trouble about that?" McCoy shook his head. "We went right to the top. If hypnoscan won't break it, then it's buried so deep nothing will. Maybe . . . time."

"Which we don't have."

"Tough universe," McCoy said wryly. "I'm more concerned right now about this business with Spock and Savaj. Jim, you can't run around trying to make yourself into a Vulcan. You're not built for it."

Kirk shook his head. "Between us, Bones, the son of a

. . . Vulcan is right. Tough universe. Nobody gives guarantees I'll be treated gently. By Romulans. By these 'experimenters.' If I could have half again my strength—"

"You'll break your neck, or your—"

"Bones, Spock's been holding back—more than I knew, more than I would have stood still for. I wish I didn't think it was even in chess."

"I don't believe *that*," McCoy said. "Maybe he plays you mostly from his Human half, now and again—which is probably good for him. But I've seen some of those psychouts of yours. And I've seen that one game he had analyzed for you—when the top grand masters of the galaxy cited you for grand master's level play."*

Kirk looked slightly mollified, reminded. "It takes me weeks to do that, one, two moves a day, if I'm lucky."

"Meanwhile, you can *do* it. You can't calculate to sixteen decimals in the time Spock can either. But he takes your orders."

Kirk grinned. "Bones, remind me to cite you for grand master's level in bedside manner."

"Your old country doctor."

"You better get out of here now before we both get in trouble."

"Get some rest, Jim." McCoy put a hand on Kirk's shoulder for a moment, then left. In the hall he stopped. The shoulder had somehow felt surprisingly vulnerable. Kirk was in training, but it was the slim training of running and swimming now, healthier, but not quite the look of power the massive shoulders had once given him. McCoy didn't want to see Kirk give what it would take out of him to get the other 60 percent.

He decided to have a talk with Spock—maybe even with Savaj. There was no way Jim could or would back down, but maybe Spock would see sense.

Savaj was something else.

---

* "Surprise," from *Star Trek: The New Voyages*, No. 2, edited by Sondra Marshak and Myrna Culbreath

Chapter Eight

During the ship's night, in one of its outphase stages, the alien ship simply vanished. Mass readings dropped to zero, and the visual did not reappear.

Spock nevertheless remained in the command chair for the rest of the night watch. It was he who saw the red line on guest quarters' life support.

He alerted Sulu, called Scott to meet him at guest quarters, and shot there by turbolift.

The corridor was freezing cold and the readout panel showed a high concentration of carbon dioxide and dangerous amounts of carbon monoxide. Scott arrived and swore, started dumping and recycling air.

Spock went to the only occupied guest cabin, signaled, got no answer, and found the door jammed by computer interlock. He placed his palms against the door, wedged fingertips into the crack, and forced it until the lock snapped.

He went in and found Savaj in a light body-trance state, metabolism slowed, the sleeping body's ingrained defense against severe Vulcan changes of temperature or pressure. But the trance state was not a defense against the carbon monoxide, to which Vulcans were particularly sensitive and without natural defense.

Spock carried Savaj to the corridor and beyond the cold line and slapped his face hard to rouse him from the trance.

McCoy was there, blinking back sleep and bending over Savaj with a scanner. He set a stimulant and detoxifier on the spray hypo and pressed it to Savaj's arm.

Suddenly Kirk was there too.

"What happened, Spock?"

Spock looked up. "You were not released." He slapped Savaj again and the Vulcan caught Spock's wrist and opened his eyes.

Savaj was completely awake and fully aware. "Life support?" he asked.

"Monoxide levels quickly lethal to a Vulcan."

"Apparently a computer error," Scott answered. "I canna understand *how*, but it's fixed now."

"Reassign to officers' quarters," Spock said, "until you *do* understand, Mr. Scott. Class One Check."

"Aye, sir. I don't like the look of the carbon monoxide."

Kirk was inspecting the readout. "That's no ordinary malfunction."

"No," Spock said, "it is not. Mr. Kirk, return to quarters. Savaj, with me." The full Vulcan gathered himself and came to his feet and the two Vulcans moved off.

Kirk turned and went to his quarters. McCoy tagged Spock and Savaj to the vacant officer's suite beside Kirk's cabin.

Savaj nodded. "I shall require no assistance."

"An enviable certainty, Admiral," Spock said. "Which regrettably I do not share. It was a most peculiar computer error. And highly selective."

"The thought had occurred, Captain. However, assistance in all probability would be superfluous or unavailing." Savaj turned and went in.

"Spock, you don't mean—" McCoy began.

Spock turned to him. "Accidents, as you will doubtless point out, do happen, Doctor. I find it disquieting when they happen in sequence and in the face of an unknown alien presence—which has possibly even affected members of this crew."

McCoy nodded. "So do I. I also find it disquieting when a less mysterious alien presence affects *you*. A Vulcan presence. Spock, you're pushing Jim too hard."

"That may be, Doctor," Spock said without expression.

"Then you'll stop?" McCoy said hopefully, a little dubiously.

"No."

"But *why*, Spock? Because some double-Vulcan sits on your neck?"

"No, Doctor. Because Savaj is *right*."

"To put Jim—and *you*—on the spot in front of your crew? To push Jim with a strength he can't match—which he'll break his anatomy trying?"

"To save his life," Spock said. "A function that a Vulcan would properly have performed for his commander. I have not."

"No more than two or three dozen times I could count. Not counting routine crises."

"Failure is counted only once, Doctor."

Spock turned. At the door to his quarters he turned back. "Has it occurred to you that Kirk would not have survived either of those accidents?" He went in without waiting for an answer.

Kirk answered the intercom. He hadn't slept since the accident to Savaj and not well before that—some kind of vague, recurrent nightmare from which he woke in a cold sweat and which he could not remember.

He'd been running computer checks from his cabin console and pacing. They were still on course back to Helvan. The computer gave no definitive answer on how the accident had happened.

"Spock here," the intercom said on audio. "You may join me on the rec deck, Mr. Kirk, if you wish. Five minutes."

"I wish," Kirk said, somewhere between fuming and forgiveness. "On my way." He pulled on the *asumi* outfit he had worn back to his quarters and moved.

The rec deck seemed to be largely populated by a crowd of mutterers. They didn't immediately notice Kirk and he had a chance to see that the center of their discontent appeared to be the message display.

He moved over to get a look but was blocked by bodies. One of them proved to be the always noteworthy one that belonged to Uhura.

"What's the revolution?" he said over her shoulder.

She turned, startled. "Cap—Captain," she finished firmly. "Good to see you, sir. You're not far wrong." She moved a little to let him see over her shoulder.

There was an order posted doubling the all-crew fitness requirement, signed by Spock.

Kirk suppressed a groan, looked at Uhura ruefully. "Sorry."

She nodded. "It *is* widely regarded as your fault, sir."

"Thanks."

"There's another popular candidate," she indicated over his left shoulder and he looked to see Savaj coming onto the rec deck.

A number of stares ranging from mildly irritated to distinctly unfriendly followed the Vulcan. Kirk felt somehow unaccountably warmed. Uhura's look was toward the distinctly unfriendly end, but he noticed that she followed the full Vulcan's catlike movement with a certain intentness that struck him as female perception of the Vulcan as exceedingly male.

"Nobody can figure him out, Captain, including me," Uhura said. "I tried to talk to him about his communications breakthrough. But *I* didn't make one. Might as well have tried it on a tree." She sighed. "Mr. Dobius," she said with satisfaction, naming the seven-foot Tanian with bifurcated head, "wants to challenge the admiral to three falls."

Kirk had to suppress a chuckle, but he managed a more-or-less straight face. "Head him off, Uhura—thanks but no thanks."

"I dinna see *why*, Captain," Scott chipped in from behind him, evidently eavesdropping shamelessly. "The Tanian is near the only one who could mix it up close to even with a Vulcan. And Dobius is none too fond of a Vulcan who would lean on a Human with that muscle. Nor am I, begging your pardon, sir. Mr. Spock is one thing. But *that* cold fish—"

Kirk turned to look at Scott. The engineer was dour-faced, worried about him. "Mr. Scott, I'm not quite a back number yet. I'll try him a fall or two myself." He put a hand to the back of his neck and grimaced ruefully. "Just as soon as I get over the last one." He let his look include those now clustering within earshot. "Meanwhile

I suggest you start figuring ways to work in Captain Spock's new fitness requirement. Very likely he'll be testing strength levels himself soon—if our visitors of last night don't do it for him."

Some of them sobered. He seized the moment and made his escape. Most of them did not know what was never far from his mind—that the full Vulcan they resented on his behalf had come close to dying last night on his ship.

Savaj was exercising alone—some exotic routine that looked a little like a Cossack dance in slow motion, but several times as tough. Kirk knew he couldn't have done it to save his life.

Kirk nodded. "Admiral."

"Mr. Kirk." Savaj did a deep knee bend—on one leg—with the other extended parallel to the floor.

Kirk set his teeth and took the plunge. "Would you teach me that, sir?"

Savaj raised an eyebrow. Vulcans were probably too polite to laugh in his face. Savaj rose, still on the single leg, then extended his hands to Kirk.

Kirk took the hands, somewhat dubiously, but firmly.

"Mirror," Savaj said.

The full Vulcan turned slightly to one side and raised a knee past Kirk's thigh. Kirk mirrored it on the opposite side. Savaj leaned back slightly, his strength a counterweight for Kirk, and they went down slowly on the opposite legs. Not that muscles did not complain, but Kirk was left little time to worry about it.

Savaj led him then through a routine he could not have begun alone—nor with another Human. With Savaj's strength and absolute balance to counterweight, guide, support, lift, it was beyond Kirk's strength, but not quite beyond some limit he could reach by transcending. It was a warrior's routine: power, grace, strength, balance, split-second timing, courage, endurance—working every muscle and nerve, the body—perhaps the soul. Characteristically the Vulcan also combined their diversities to form beauty.

Savaj worked it so that the toughest strength moves were his—a high lift, Kirk extending rigid arms against Savaj's and being lifted, turned above the Vulcan's head and down again into the crossed circle of wrists, then back up into a reverse. A roll, Kirk shoulder-rolling over

65

the Vulcan's back. A carry, Kirk lifted by one stirrup hand to the Vulcan's shoulders, then above his head, effortlessly. Finally up into a handstand on the Vulcan's hand.

Savaj choreographed the routine. He must have been guiding, telegraphing the movements to Kirk with his hands, his eyes, his body—although Kirk had no awareness of that. He merely seemed to know what to do. But a Vulcan wouldn't plant that knowing in his mind, surely. There was no time to think about it. Savaj did a vault over Kirk's shoulders, allowing him to support part of his weight for a moment. then finished with another power lift and brought him down to the starting position.

After a moment Savaj disengaged, bowed his head faintly. "Lesson one."

"Thank you, sir," Kirk said.

"Unnecessary."

Kirk realized that they had drawn a crowd again. He had not really been aware of it while they moved. Now he saw a kind of startled attention in the eyes, as if they had seen something extraordinary. Kirk was something of a gymnast. He knew he had never done anything of the kind. He wondered if any Human had.

"Sir, you lift me as if I were—not even a child. A child's doll."

Savaj shrugged an eyebrow. "You must realize, Captain, that I am equipped to lift a full-grown Vulcan of heavier bone and denser muscle in the heavier gravity of Vulcan —and possibly carry him up cliffs or out of the teeth of the *le matya*. You are no great feat. The analogy of a mere plaything is somewhat figurative, but essentially correct."

Kirk found himself silenced, for once. And it was a moment before he realized that he had heard Savaj call him Captain. He did not think that Vulcans made mistakes of that kind.

"Few playthings, however, can read and execute a *T'hyvaj*." The Vulcan bowed fractionally. "My pleasure."

"Mine," Kirk said. "Tomorrow?" But he suddenly looked beyond the crowd and saw a solitary figure waiting on an exercise mat. Spock.

"If you will excuse me, Admiral," Kirk said, and went to Spock.

"Perhaps you are fatigued by the *T'hyvaj*," Spock said.

Kirk tried his best scapegrace look. "Dead. Never felt better. Ready to take on my weight in *le matyas*."

"That would be a very small *le matya*."

"A kitten," Kirk said. "That ought to be just about right."

Spock shook his head. "Unhatched."

Kirk sighed. He stepped onto the mat and bowed. They locked arms.

"Why did you never teach me the *T'hyvaj*, Spock?"

"I cannot say. It is a thing one may learn from the ancient path."

"Of warriors?"

Spock nodded. "Of *T'hy'la* from before the dawn of our days. Are you prepared?"

Kirk tried to clear his head and set himself for the *asumi*. "I am prepared," he answered correctly.

But he was not, or it would have done him no good if he were. Spock took him down as effortlessly as Savaj had lifted him. Then again. Kirk was getting a little tired of this particular diversity.

Then he put his back into it and his mind on it and got in a flying scissors fall.

Somebody cheered. He glanced at them warningly.

But it was the last time he put Spock down. The Vulcan began to handle him not for a fall, but to force maximum resistance, build maximum strength.

After five minutes he felt as if he had been trying to move all of Vulcan. Which was approximately the case. It was the technique of the tree. One imagined oneself rooted in the planet; who moves me moves my world. Spock had a vivid imagination.

Kirk backed off finally and made the lesser signal for "Enough."

"Captain Spock, I feel freshly overhauled and thoroughly demoralized. Do you think we could find such a thing as breakfast?"

Spock lifted an eyebrow. "You have my permission to report to the bridge after making the attempt." He moved off toward the turbolift, still wearing the *asumi* outfit, leaving Kirk flatfooted.

Pavel Chekov had scared up a cup of coffee somewhere

and came over to put it in Kirk's hand. "Mr. Spock seems to be taking all this very seriously, sair."

"Thank you, Pavel," Kirk said, but he could not let that pass. "In some three hours, Mr. Chekov, we will be in orbit of Helvan again. By the looks of you, if nothing else, that warrants some taking seriously." The Russian was pale, suddenly gaunt. "How have you been sleeping?"

Chekov shrugged. "Sleep? I seem to remember that was invented by a little old Russian lady from—"

"You haven't."

"Certainly not if I can help it. And not long. The nightmares—"

"Can you remember them?"

"*Nyet*. Nothing. Just that I want to get my hands on somebody—"

"Report to Dr. McCoy, Mr. Chekov, and get a REM cycle of sleep. I'll tell Captain Spock."

Chekov shook his head. "Thank you, Captain, but I'm counting on making that landing party."

"There's time, Mr. Chekov. Otherwise you won't be in shape for it. Go."

"Yes, sair."

"Pavel—I know how you feel."

Chekov grinned and left. Kirk settled for the coffee, a sonic scrub, and a clothes change, not in the closed cubicles, and headed for the bridge.

Chapter Nine

Three hours later they were in orbit of Helvan. Communications and scanner reports from the planet's surface were not encouraging. Conditions had deteriorated rapidly. A full-scale revolution was in progress. Disappearances were increasing. Panic and mob violence were sweeping the planet.

Kirk slipped away unobtrusively to have McCoy give him horns again—only to find Chapel artistically completing the job for McCoy.

"Bones, Spock hasn't called you for the landing party."

McCoy snorted. "He hasn't called anybody. Including *you*. Business has been brisk. Come here."

Shortly Kirk had his horns. It began to strike him as ominous that Spock had never shed his.

The intercom bleeped. Rand's voice came over it. "Mr. Spock has alerted the transporter room for beamdown—five minutes."

Kirk and McCoy moved out fast. They found Uhura in the transporter room staunchly rigged out with full field kit for communications. Chekov was there with a small belt arsenal and standard issue weapons for the party, wearing a rather grim look under his horns.

Spock came in, took in their presence at a glance.

Savaj came in behind him. Rand caught an audible breath. If they had ever accused Spock of looking like the devil himself, they had been mistaken. *This* was the Son of Darkness, made flesh. The horns merely completed the image, but the Vulcan face was carved from legend, dream, nightmare—his dark Satanic majesty. If there were a face that would have stood against God, this was the face.

Spock looked at the assembled party, nodded. "Commendable zeal. Thank you. However, the landing party will consist only of those who are immune to the effect." He turned to Kirk. "A principle of logic and of command that I have commended to you on several occasions. Notably against the cloud-creature—"

"Spock, do you know what you can do with that cloud—" Kirk cut himself off. "Captain Spock, we are not here to remain safe on the ship—assuming that that *is* safe, which is doubtful. We are here to study the alien effect. Immunity does not necessarily draw it—while *we* obviously do. Immunity may not detect it—while our rapport *did*. That's what this crew is *here* for."

"Mr. Kirk, not until and unless all the alternatives that can be explored by two Vulcans have been exhausted. We need no detection to know that the effect is operating on this planet. You have already drawn it—only too successfully. It has had its chance at you. As for rapport, it served only to detect the effect. If there is immunity, there is no effect to detect."

"Even *that* is not established, Spock. Vulcan immunity is an assumption. And *you* are half Human."

"That is a matter of record," Spock said. "As is the fact that I am in command of this ship. For your information, Mr. Kirk, there is no case on record in which someone has disappeared—twice—and returned. I will give this no second chance at previous victims and no Human victims at all until the power of Vulcan has been tried against it. If Savaj or I are taken, as Vulcans we stand some significant probability of extricating ourselves or of learning the nature of the enemy."

He turned to face Kirk directly.

"Hear this, Mr. Kirk. I am leaving you the con, against my better judgment. But I am leaving you under strict orders, per all applicable Starfleet regulations. In the event

70

that the landing party disappears, appears to be in trouble, or does not return, you are to mount no rescue mission, allow no one to leave the ship, make no attempt of any kind at rescue. If out of contact for more than four hours, you are to log landing party expended and leave orbit at once for Vulcan—and not to return without a full complement of Vulcans under a Vulcan Command Officer."

"Spock," Kirk said carefully, "you are asking me to 'expend' not only an officer and friend who is invaluable to Starfleet and indispensable to me, but also a ranking flag officer of Starfleet, Admiral Savaj, one of the premier minds of the galaxy."

"No, Mr. Kirk. I am not *asking*," Spock said flatly. "That is a binding final order of a command officer knowingly going into a potential no-return situation. It leaves you no options, no judgment call. I so log it now. You will answer to Starfleet. Or, should I survive, to *me*." He turned to mount the transporter with Savaj.

"Or, should I, to me," Savaj added.

"Energize," Spock said.

Kirk said nothing.

But he looked at Spock with the look that Spock would be able to read as "In a pig's eye."

He narrowly restrained himself from saying it aloud, by telling himself that Spock would come beaming back to deal with him now—and to relieve him of the con.

As it was, Spock would leave the command to him for that edge of intuition and command judgment that Spock knew to be his and that might well be needed to save the ship. Spock knew well enough that, when push came to shove, having to answer to Starfleet would not stop Kirk.

McCoy's look at Kirk speculated on whether having to answer to Spock or Savaj *would*.

"You know, Jim, they don't necessarily have to be bound by Human-oriented Starfleet regs. They're entitled to Vulcan diversity in that too. Vulcan wing and command code."

Kirk made a rueful face. "Bones, you could have talked all day without saying that."

McCoy harumphed. "Listen, I *saw* Vulcan diversity, remember? T'Pring got to be *property* in a Vulcan second for challenging a marriage agreement made by her parents when she was seven. What do you figure a Vulcan *ship*

71

does to an officer who breaks a Starfleet oath sworn as an adult?"

"Bones," Kirk said, "you better go conjure up a spell against our ever having to find out. You really figure I'm going to up ship and leave them there if they get into trouble?"

McCoy sighed. "I'll go haul out my eye of newt." He started to turn. "But, Jim, maybe Spock has a point. If only Vulcans can deal with this—and even our *judgment* is affected—"

"Even *mine*. I know, Bones. It's still the only judgment I've got." Kirk turned to Scott at the transporter controls.

"I want a full life form reading tracking scan on them at all times."

"Aye, sir," Scott said. "But they're already in the thick of it."

Kirk was there in three strides. The two Vulcan life forms were surrounded by a mob.

Spock and Savaj had beamed down into a deserted alley.

Spock tried his communicator. It had been a mistake to leave Kirk the con. Spock knew that look.

Not that there had been, in fact, much choice. Given what Kirk was, there was little short of sedation or incarceration which would stop him from taking command of that ship if the landing party were lost. Nor was there anyone on the ship who would not back Kirk if he did.

Spock had bowed to that logic, and it had, nevertheless, been a mistake.

"Spock to *Enterprise*."

No answer. No signal, Spock determined momentarily.

"Jammed," Savaj confirmed, trying his own. "Of little use to relieve him in any case."

Spock suppressed an almost Human irritation at being read so exactly. "You believe I am remiss in *Tzaled*."

"No. I observe it."

"Observation noted."

"You have permitted superior judgment to be subordinated to the lesser."

"He has been my commander."

"You are his natural superior."

"That thought has occasionally occurred. However,

there is a beyond-level to the complex fact which you have had no opportunity to observe."

Savaj shrugged. "The more reason for that *Tzaled* level of loyalty to commander. It would in this case require that kind of subadult instruction which is owed to an erratically brilliant and dangerous child prodigy."

Spock nodded. "I commend to you, Admiral, the task of attempting to do so with a Human Beethoven—or a Kirk."

Spock moved quietly to the mouth of the alley, Savaj following.

What had been a relatively quiet street suddenly filled with a mob. It swirled around them and suddenly swept them up into it—a raging torrent of horned beings.

They attempted to work out to the edge of it, but suddenly it swept around a corner and jammed them into a crowd of thousands watching as an armed party attacked the Summer Palace. They found slight shelter by a stone column.

Spock saw peasants assaulting the palace with pitchforks. He saw the powder and shot tubes that had been a new object of curiosity here only days ago. And now he saw also well-developed muzzle loaders. Another new party dashed forward, some waving new breechloaders that took a rough cartridge.

"Centuries of gunsmithing," Spock said. "Within days."

Savaj nodded. "The revolution proceeding here is by my reckoning four centuries too early and compressing three hundred years of revolution into a matter of weeks. Unfortunately it is in grave danger of compressing the great liberating revolutions of the normal Richter scale with the later antilife, authoritarian revolutions."

"You have studied the planet," Spock said.

"Three years ago. Stagnant, prescientific—in early feudalism, with none of the seeds of this change within it."

"You are saying, sociological experimentation," Spock divined.

"Yes," Savaj said. "But much more than that." He indicated he was already scanning with the palmed readout scanner of his tricorder.

Spock did the same. Reasonably normal. Then he noted something which made him take a second look.

Since they had arrived, a wing of the palace had fallen

to the rebels. Banners had been brought up, a cannon. Leaders organized impromptu groups that moved fast to sudden objectives. Spock finally placed the subliminal feeling that was nagging at him.

It was as if they were watching from a slow-motion film, while the Helvan real world speeded past them. But it was not so much the physical world that had speeded up.

"Time——" Spock began. "No. Psychological time?"

Savaj nodded. "It is a speed increment of a natural phenomenon. There are certain periods on all worlds when a century does the work of a millennium—only to be followed by a decade that does the work of a century. But now, on this and other worlds, the year becomes the millennium. But not without outside help."

Suddenly someone in the crowd turned, noting the strange instruments in their hands—and suddenly a horned Helvan male snarled like a mad thing and came at them. Contagion caught the crowd and a sudden horned tidal wave swept toward them.

Savaj caught Spock's arm and they ran. Quarry. They were the hunted, now. Whether they knew it or not, these people must sense the presence of the experimenters—and now identified Spock and Savaj with that presence. The Helvan response was the wish to tear their throats out.

They dodged around buildings and over walls until they seemed to have lost the pursuit. Savaj had given Spock a flying heave up a three-man height wall and leaped up to catch Spock's hand and swing himself over as Spock lifted him. It was perhaps the first time in twenty-odd years that Spock had been the one to be assisted by a strength to match or exceed his own.

They ducked into a narrow alcove while a contingent of Helvans pounded past.

"This, then, has been your decade," Spock said.

Savaj nodded. "It has been my life. But certainly my decade. I began to notice it long ago. There is a pattern of anomalies that represents some grand design. The designers remain unknown. It is beyond the capacity of any known life form in this galaxy. It appears to include matched planet samples, sophisticated experimental design, and a supreme willingness to pay the price of knowledge —in other life forms' lives."

"To investigate what hypothesis?" Spock said.

"Unknown. The intent is perhaps not malevolent. Nor is it benevolent. Some changes are destructive, dangerous; some may be beneficial. However, the alien action amounts to a supreme disregard of any principle of noninterference. It is the antithesis of our Federation's own Prime Directive of nonintervention. The Designers' directive is: Always intervene."

Spock looked at him narrowly. "But you do have some theory as to the experimental hypothesis."

Savaj's eyes studied him. "I do. However, it remains so improbable that I have no logical evidence to support it. I prefer to reserve it until we have gathered evidence."

"I have found," Spock said, "that it frequently expedites the process of gathering evidence to share even what Humans would regard as unfounded speculation."

"We are not Human, Spock." Savaj consulted his tricorder. "There is a power source bearing Thirteen Mark Three that is not compatible even with the new Helvan rate of advance." He gestured to Spock to move out and Spock moved around the Helvan burdenbeasts tethered by the alley.

It was at that point that all the instruments agreed with Savaj of Vulcan: Captain Spock walked around the burdenbeasts—and disappeared.

Savaj checked the communicator, found it still useless, and set off on bearing 13 Mark 3.

Chapter Ten

Kirk turned from his transporter room computer check in sudden alarm. He could not have defined the source of the feeling. Some sense of Spock's presence seemed to have cut out.

A few minutes ago Scott's life form tracking had shown Spock and Savaj elude immediate pursuit and gain a place of apparent safety. The pursuit had been Helvan—dangerous but not mysterious. Yet Kirk had still felt a nagging sense of severe unease that seemed to go beyond the immediate danger.

A thought came to him and he stepped back to the transporter room main computer link to run still another check on the accident to Savaj's life-support system and the computer failure that had turned Spock's changing cubicle into a near-lethal death trap. Spock had said that monoxide was quickly fatal to Vulcans; Savaj, that asphyxiation and pressure were. There were not very many things on a Human ship to which a Vulcan was severely vulnerable.

This time Kirk asked the computer for the probability of two such accidental random computer failures in close sequence, involving hazards particularly lethal to the only two Vulcans aboard. What was the probability that they *were* accidents?

"Probability approximates zero," the computer answered dispassionately.

Kirk felt a sudden chill. On a ship where at least four Humans had been exposed to some alien mind-altering effect, two separate attempts had been made on the lives of the only two aboard who might be immune to that effect.

He started to run a program. "Persons capable of necessary computer alteration."

But it was at that moment that he had the sense of something more immediately wrong. His legs started to buckle. The fury, terror, shame, swept over him—a more volcanic fury than his own and a deeper shame at experiencing terror.

"*Spock,*" Kirk said aloud.

"Nay, Captain," Scott said in sudden alarm. "I just lost him."

Kirk tried to get some sense of the direction the feeling came from, but it suddenly whited out in an incandescent burst of pain.

He found Scott balancing him as he faltered. He cleared his head and moved to read the life form scan. It showed one full Vulcan life form proceeding in a straight line. The other reading, Spock's, had vanished.

"Kirk to Spock," Kirk said into the communicator. "Kirk to Savaj." Nothing.

"Widen scan." Scott switched to wider map coordinates, which still flagged no other Vulcan life form. "This?" Kirk said, stabbing a finger at a bright spot on the display.

"Power source of some kind, Captain," Scott said. "Seems to have had a surge just now."

The straight line of Savaj's progress pointed in the direction of the power source.

"Beam me down, pinpoint, inside there." Kirk tapped the bright spot.

"Sir, I canna do that. Ye heard what Spock said. Even Starfleet will have your command—he left Admiral Nogura no way out. And if *Spock* himself comes back—"

"Mr. Scott, if Spock doesn't come back, or if Savaj doesn't, Nogura can take my command and—"

"Beggin' your pardon, sir, but it's Mr. Spock I'd worry about if I were you. Or that other one."

"I *am*, Scotty. Beam me down." He was gathering two phasers.

"It's on auto," Scott said, motioning a technician to the transporter console and grabbing another phaser. "I'm goin' wi' ye."

"No, Mr. Scott. I'm not going to risk anyone else against those alien effects. There's some chance for a quick one-man smash and grab, in and out. If you can't beam us out within three and a half hours, follow Spock's order." He mounted the transporter. Scott reluctantly returned to the controls. *"Now,* Scotty."

Scott gave him a look that also put Kirk's last order in the ocular organ of a porcine omnivore.

Kirk emerged in some space where the light was wrong for his eyes, the shapes wrong for his body, the screeches unendurable to his ears.

The sights were so appalling that his eyes virtually refused to take anything in. But he did see aliens of some unknown and inexplicably horrifying kind—mouthless, yet they screamed.

No. *They* did not scream.

Now he could see naked humanoids, Helvans, perhaps some others, strapped down to tables with metal bands. His eyes balked. Unspeakable things were being done by the no-mouths to the helpless victims, without the slightest sign from the no-mouths of concern or even awareness of the horror. Some of the humanoids were merely being examined. Some were being altered. Some had caustic fluids dripping into their eyes.

What perhaps horrified Kirk most was that he was certain it was not sadism. There was not even that much empathy with what the victims felt. There was not even the satisfaction of torturers in these no-mouths. Mere, utter indifference.

Experimenters, Kirk thought. What if that was exactly it? A laboratory technician might vivisect a lab dog and then go home and play with his pet dog.

Then Kirk saw Spock spread-eagled to a table, no-mouths bending over him. His eyes found Kirk with incandescent fury.

The no-mouths were rushing Kirk now, and he cut a path toward Spock with both phasers firing on heavy stun. The no-mouths were resistant, but finally fell. They climbed over each other and kept coming. They came from behind him.

He reached Spock and turned to defend the Vulcan, mowing them down.

"T'Vareth!" Spock snarled. "Disobedient fool-whelp."

The no-mouths were closing in. Kirk tried to signal the *Enterprise.* No luck.

Suddenly Spock found the strength he had not found for himself. In one convulsive heave he snapped the metal bands that bound him and gained his feet. For a long moment he flailed around him with great double-handed Vulcan chops that piled damaged no-mouths at their feet. He reached Kirk.

They fought shoulder to shoulder, sometimes back to back, Spock cutting a path toward a door. Kirk found a fierce grin on his face, compounded of terror and all the times they had beaten the thousands-to-one odds before.

This time they did not. New reinforcements of no-mouths climbed over fallen ones and kept coming until even the Vulcan was buried in them.

Kirk blacked out on the knowledge that they had both fallen into the hands of utter evil.

He awoke strapped down, metal biting into wrists, ankles. Dispassionate alien hands probed at him. He was face down. For a long moment he could see nothing. Then he managed to turn his head and saw Spock, strapped on another table beside him, conscious of everything being done to or prepared for either of them.

The no-mouths were handling Kirk as if he were an inanimate object. No. Worse. As if he were an animate one whose feelings were of no concern. Terror, shame, agony, rage, mute appeal, intelligence, logic—instinctively he knew that nothing would reach them.

This was a callousness so profound that it did not even know itself for callousness. It had desensitized itself to any empathy. Kirk knew that he had never been so terrified in his life.

Then something wrenched at his mind and he screamed.

No. That was not true. Now he knew the source of the shame. He had been here once before. . . .

Scott beamed down with McCoy and the largest armed party he had ever mounted from the *Enterprise*—Chekov supervising weapons deployment, Uhura, Rand, and Chapel showing up with an insistent contingent of volunteers—virtually everyone on board who was not bolted to a duty station. They had heard that Kirk had gone after Spock and been caught.

Scott had warned this could be a suicide mission—and a court-martial offense. Nobody seemed to bat an eye.

Scott didn't stop to argue. By his latest readings the place was crawling with unclassifiable alien life forms—but there were also humanoid readings, some of them in agony. Two of those humanoids were his own. It was war.

Now armed parties were popping down by auxiliary transporter in groups of six.

There was, Scott had decided, no question of the Prime Directive. Whatever those beasties in the power installation were, they weren't Helvan, and they definitely weren't primitive. But they *were* savages. Those pain readings! McCoy's face had gone white.

Scott signaled to his immediate party and crept up through the underbrush toward the alien installation's power field. He had gotten Kirk in with a pinpoint single transporter beam, but it had proved impossible to beam him out.

Something rose out of the ground in front of Scott—a horned apparition.

"Mr. Scott," it said.

If it wasn't the devil himself—

"This way," Savaj said, and began signaling to the landing party contingents—circle here, attack there, take that high point, that autosentry—*now!*

It was all done silently and as if Savaj had been doing it for a hundred years.

Which, Scott figured, he probably *had*.

It was only as they charged, unquestioningly, on the Vulcan's order that it came home to Scott that this *was* a full Vulcan—schooled in the absolute of a thousand years' peace.

But the still-older ancestral Vulcan warrior had come out.

There was certainly neither peace nor pacifism in the Vulcan's face. He might have been a Vulcan berserker from the dawn of time. And yet that savage fighting machine was still guided by the great Vulcan brain. They seemed to hit every vulnerable point on this side of the installation at once—phaser armor-piercers breaching the walls, phaser rifles and sidearms cutting down the opposition on heavy stun.

The Vulcan led the point, and often as not he merely smashed his way through the neckless, mouthless gray aliens—picking up one and heaving it to bowl down others.

Scott tried it. The beastie things didn't seem very big. The one he tried must have been bolted to the floor. He got it with the phaser just as its clawlike hands went for his eyes.

It was impossible not to feel that the things were evil.

Then he saw Kirk. The claw-handed things were still working over him, not responding to the attack, assuming others would deal with it.

Scott's stomach turned over. He heaved a gray-thing over after all and charged. Then he saw Spock, double-bound to a table, suddenly withdraw into himself and put all his life force into one arm. It cut itself against the bands, then snapped them. The arm swept out and knocked three no-mouths down and away from Kirk's table. Another move and Spock's hand shot Kirk's rolling table away from the other no-mouths and toward Savaj.

The full Vulcan broke through the opposition, caught Kirk's table, snapped Kirk's bonds with his hands, and gathered the half-conscious Kirk into one arm, bracing him on uncertain legs.

More no-mouths burst in from another direction, cutting the rescue party and Kirk off from Spock.

"Back!" Spock ordered. "Out! *Now!*"

But Savaj was already moving to cut through to Spock, one-handed, the other arm still bracing Kirk—Scott, McCoy, Chekov, and Rand forming a flying wedge behind them.

Kirk shook his head, trying to clear it, saw Spock, and began to help beat a way through the attackers. He was out on his feet, but in some way some of the *asumi* moves Scott had seen him practice with the Vulcans were coming through.

They reached Spock and Savaj ripped him free.

Scott heaved Spock to his feet and could virtually hear Vulcan rage crackling around him. "I said, *'Out!'*" Spock snapped.

And, indeed, Scott saw that the last push to get to the Vulcan had left them surrounded, cut off by overwhelming force. No chance of beaming out from under the power field. No way they were going to get out now at all. . . .

Kirk fought for consciousness. He knew he was moving, fighting, functioning, and that he was neither conscious nor sane.

There was some depth of rage in him that would have annihilated every no-mouth thing in the galaxy, would have pulled the galaxy down on top of them if it killed him.

He waded in to start on the job.

He was aware of Savaj, still bracing him intermittently or trying to cover him from close attack.

Then it filtered through to Kirk on some level that was still sane that his immediate *Enterprise* party was completely surrounded and its position was quite hopeless.

Hundreds of no-mouths, some of them using animal-control devices now, had cut the Vulcans, Kirk, McCoy, Chekov, Rand, Uhura, Dobius off from the rest of the *Enterprise* landing force.

In moments they would be buried in sheer numbers. He saw Spock, alive, naked, fighting the no-months to deadly effect, but without logical hope of escape. Savaj, also, was selling their lives dear, but without reasonable doubt of the inevitable outcome.

Kirk saw no out himself. But he had never bought that as a policy. Without much thought he found himself climbing up over fallen no-mouths and finally up onto the solidly packed shoulders of standing ones and toward the breakthrough point they had to reach.

He would be pulled down in a moment. But he looked back and saw what some instinct told him would be the effect. The two Vulcans moved as one. Spock began chopping into the no-mouths with great double-handed blows that no flesh could stand against. Savaj picked up a no-mouth and used it as a battering ram. The giant Dobius followed his example. Rand stiff-armed the cone-noses with the heel of her hand. Scott found some way of heaving them over, and McCoy was making some effort to come up over the top after Kirk.

Kirk wasn't sure whether they were madder at the no-mouths or at him. Either concept suited him for the moment, so long as they came after him.

Clawed hands were pulling him down when they reached him. Savaj bulldozed him forward over the top, and suddenly they were through. They linked with the main *Enterprise* party trying to reach them and all made for daylight.

"Take a prisoner," Kirk croaked, and saw Dobius hear him and pick up a no-mouth by the scruff of the neck it did not have.

Kirk himself was barely on his feet, was being bundled forward, off and on, by Savaj, Spock, or McCoy, who was muttering, "Fool stunt."

"Got you," Kirk managed without breath. "For a doctor you make a pretty fair berserker."

"You haven't seen anything yet," McCoy snapped warningly.

Groups were being picked up by transporter while they covered the rear.

Finally the shimmer picked them up, the last group, as a new wave of no-mouths poured over the position they beamed out of.

Kirk collapsed neatly onto his knees on the *Enterprise* transporter platform.

They seemed to be all over him. Doctors, med-techs, Vulcans.

Somebody had produced a grav-stretcher blanket. He gathered that and his dignity around him, what was left of it, and got to his feet. He considered it a major accomplishment.

Spock also was on his feet—not steadily, but his Vulcan mode was in working order. Without thought his hands deftly produced some Vulcan fold-and-tuck arrangement with one of the light medical coverlets that made it look like the perfectly groomed uniform of the day.

The thought and the baleful look he reserved for a

somewhat bedraggled Human who achieved no such elegance. "Mr. Kirk, you are relieved of duty and authority pending further action."

"Understood," Kirk managed.

"Mr. Scott, you will show cause why I shall not also cite you for gross insubordination and mutiny."

Kirk cut Scott off. "It was *my* responsibility."

"You have none," Spock said glacially.

"Your binding order by chain of command ends with me," Kirk said firmly. "If Mr. Scott has anything to answer for, it is to me." Privately his eyes made a note of that for Scott.

Spock ignored him. "Mr. Scott, return to duty pending decision. Guards, take Mr. Kirk to the security section of Sick Bay." Two security guards hesitated, then moved in beside Kirk.

"Take him to main Sick Bay," McCoy snapped. "Damn it, Spock—"

"Doctor," Spock said, freezing him with a look, "as of this moment and retroactive to my assumption of command, this ship is under Vulcan rule of command."

"*What* Vulcan rule?" McCoy said dangerously.

"Instant, unqualified, unargued obedience."

"Spock," McCoy said, "this is an all-worlds ship, under uniform Starfleet code, subject to predominance of Humans and favoring best Human naval exploration tradition."

Spock took McCoy's arm—not harshly, but very firmly —and moved him toward the door. "Not when I command, Doctor." McCoy looked down at the Vulcan's grip on his arm, shocked. It was not something Spock, in ordinary mode, would have done. "A Vulcan commands in Vulcan mode, pursuant to the treaty that resolved the then Vulcan Fleet Commander's early objection to formation of a United Federation and Starfleet."

"Don't cite me the then Vulcan Fleet Commander, Spock. I wouldn't know him if I tripped over him."

"A distinct and immediate probability, Doctor." Spock steered McCoy around Savaj.

McCoy blinked, gave Savaj a long look. "*You* were the V'Kreeth?"

"That is irrelevant to your duties, Doctor," Savaj said blandly.

Kirk turned from the security person who was not so much guarding as supporting him.

"The Shadow Commander," he said in some awe.

McCoy also knew the legend. He drew himself up stoutly. "V'Kreeth Savaj, on this ship in medical matters *my* rule prevails, or you will replace me as Chief Medical Officer."

Savaj merely looked at him. "At need, I will. Attend the patient."

They had arrived at the security Sick Bay. Spock indicated a force-barred cubicle for Kirk and one for Dobius's alien prisoner.

McCoy started to balk, but Kirk caught his arm and drew him over the threshold to the diagnostic couch.

"I'm not going to argue while I have a patient in unknown condition," McCoy began. "But—"

Savaj cut off the "but." "Nor at all. Proceed."

McCoy hissed a spray hypo into Kirk's arm before Kirk could protest. "He needs rest now."

McCoy turned and advanced toward Spock. "Now—*you.*" The Vulcan's eyes were on the medical readouts over Kirk's head. He seemed to find them adequate. He froze McCoy with a look.

"I shall deal with my medical condition in the Vulcan manner, Doctor. First, I will see to the ship and interrogate the alien prisoner. After which you will have this prisoner ready to answer charges in the Vulcan mode."

Spock turned on a heel and Savaj followed him out.

"I don't need rest, Bones," Kirk complained. "I need a bomb shelter."

"What do you think I tried to *give* you? Not that I don't have a couple of photon torpedoes for you myself. You had to go *alone,* did you? And that last fool stunt?"

Kirk shrugged, a hint of rueful apology. Finally McCoy came and examined him more thoroughly in the old manner of the country doctor, and there was more healing in Leonard McCoy's hands than in the hypo. Kirk found himself shaking again, his body violently trying to throw off some of the effect of whatever the aliens had done to him, now and before.

"Bones, I've wanted to kill. I don't think I've ever wanted to annihilate, extirpate, wipe some whole enemy kind off the face of the galaxy." He fought not to be violently ill. "I do *now*."

McCoy looked toward the cubicle that held the captured alien. "So do *I*."

"Are we wrong, Bones? A hundred times—no, more than that—we've tried to understand some alien or enemy —communicate, change their minds—or even our own. Make terms. Make peace. Live together. Now—"

"Does the cow make terms with the butcher?" McCoy said.

Kirk locked his hands together to stop the shaking. "I wish you hadn't put it quite that way, Bones."

"Me, too. Jim, get some sleep—and you'd better dream up some way for the lamb to make peace with a couple of Vulcan *snarth*."

Kirk shook his head. "I'll be hanged for a sheep, Bones. I'm not even innocent this time. Hell, I haven't got a leg to stand on. Guilty as charged. And I'd do it again. How am I supposed to explain the 'logic' of that to a couple of double-Vulcans?"

McCoy snorted. "Spock knows. Not that it will do you any good. Three years back on Vulcan—plus Savaj on his neck. I think he's really reverted this time. Jim, didn't the *V'Kreeth* open up a whole quadrant of space—and single-handedly attempt to keep Vulcan from joining in forming the Federation? I thought he must be dead."

Kirk shrugged. "Evidently that thought was somewhat premature, Bones. No Vulcan's Starfleet record goes back beyond the treaty—by rule of Vulcan privacy. Savaj's record starts then—as full admiral. The *V'Kreeth* was known to the Federation only by that name—also the name of his legendary exploration ship. It was his position that Vulcans should not serve jointly with Humans and other Federation species, nor in positions that would force them to be under the command of a Human or other less advanced species, where the Vulcan might be forced into moral compromise. Hence Starfleet's all-Vulcan ships, like the *Intrepid*. The treaty did not prohibit a Vulcan from serving on an integrated ship voluntarily. But Spock was the first—and you know his father didn't speak to him for eighteen years."

"What ever happened to Vulcan Infinite Diversity in Infinite Combinations?" McCoy grumbled.

Kirk felt himself beginning to fade again. "I think the *V'Kreeth* argued there was no conflict. It was not prejudice —merely fact, a logical recognition of diverse nature and natural superiority. It would be unjust to subordinate the greater to the lesser."

"Where have we heard *that* before?—and on how many battlefields?"

Kirk nodded. "Except—he also argued Vulcan's thousand-year peace against our much more recent savagery— and still possible lapses. He had a point. Bones, how would you really feel if you were Spock and could calculate circles around any of us, read minds, control emotions, heal yourself, follow the discipline of peace—but toss us like children if you chose—and yet somebody asked you to take *my* orders?"

McCoy pursed his lips. "More to the point is, how did *Spock* feel about it? Which is, damn glad to do it, most of the time."

"Which *was*, Bones. I never heard the end of the damn cloud-creature. What do you think he's going to do about *this?*"

But Kirk found his eyes closing, beyond his will. Dimly he knew that McCoy put a hand on his arm and stayed with him.

Chapter Eleven

Kirk marched stiffly down the corridor to Spock's quarters. McCoy had patched him up sufficiently, with a compression spray-dressing to brace some bent ribs and a few other odds and ends. There didn't seem to be a spray-splint for broken sleep or a medicine for nightmare.

Now Kirk had been summoned to the Captain's quarters, under guard. The security guards eyed him in consternation, but did their duty. McCoy marched resolutely off his right shoulder, uninvited by Spock, but not budging.

The security party signaled at the door.

"*K'vath,*" Spock's voice said. The door opened and the security lieutenant ushered Kirk inside.

The Vulcan's cabin looked like an anteroom of hell. It had again been decorated, after Spock's return to the refitted *Enterprise,* in the deep red of Spock's Vulcan preference. The weapons collection had been reinstated on the wall in remembrance of Vulcan's savage past. The attunement flame again cast flickering light and shadow from the demonic sculpture carved to house it. Of the flame-sculpture's true purpose only a few had dared to ask. But if the gargoyle had been set to guard the gates of hell, no one would have been surprised.

Now, with the two Vulcans still wearing the horns of

Helvan and the look of guarding the gates themselves, the Vulcan rendition of Human nightmare was complete.

Kirk stepped forward and gave formal greeting in the Vulcan manner.

Spock remained seated and did not return it. He looked at Kirk as if he inspected some miscreant brought before him in disgrace. "Doctor, you will absent yourself from these proceedings," Spock said flatly.

"I have the right to be here. I am his doctor—and his friend. Also *yours*, damn it."

Spock said nothing, nodded to the security men to escort McCoy out. The guards hesitated fractionally.

"By uniform code, I am entitled to counsel of my choice," Kirk said. "McCoy is my choice."

"By Vulcan code, logic speaks for itself," Spock said. "Security, remove the doctor and wait outside."

This time the security team responded to the direct order —with apologetic looks to McCoy and Kirk. On Kirk's signal McCoy set his teeth and went out with them, not to make it worse for Kirk.

The door closed behind McCoy and Kirk was alone with the Vulcans.

"*T'vareth*," Spock said dispassionately.

Kirk resisted an impulse to shift his feet, as if he were indeed called on the carpet before Spock.

"Captain Spock, I unquestionably disobeyed your order, for which I apologize. In my judgment it became neces—"

"You will not speak without permission."

Kirk bit off a protest. "Permission to speak?" he asked.

"Denied."

Kirk felt his own temper rising. "Logic speaks for itself, you said."

"Silence!"

Kirk straightened and remained silent.

"Logic speaks," Spock said. "Innocence defends. Guilt merely presents itself for justice."

"Even guilt has its reason," Kirk risked. "You would be dead."

Spock rose from the desk and looked as if he would come through it. "My life was mine to risk and mine to extricate, if possible. Has it occurred to you what we might have learned if the experimenters had continued to work

90

on me, alone, against trained Vulcan capacities to resist and remember?"

Kirk let himself show that it had not occurred to him that in Vulcan mode Spock and/or Savaj might have dispassionately put themselves in a position to be taken by the experimenters and been quite prepared to endure whatever happened, possibly even death, on the chance of learning something.

And would Spock, with that iron constitution—and with the mental disciplines that Kirk had seen defeat the Klingon mind-sifter,* plus the healing disciplines he could use—have survived long enough to learn something vital? Perhaps to transmit it to Savaj?

Maybe Kirk *had* screwed that up.

Then his mind flashed the picture of what the no-mouths were doing or about to do to Spock when he came. Kirk shook his head. "No. It didn't occur. At some point such sacrifice might buy a galaxy—or be unavoidable. Not then."

"The judgment was not yours to make," Spock said.

"Nor should it ever *have* been," Savaj said.

Spock's eyes seemed to harden in agreement. "Your species, with whatever effort, has never understood the diversity of mine. Out of respect for your diversity, I have not fully used Vulcan command mode, even when in command for some position or period. Now we cannot afford the luxury of such restraint. Full Vulcan command mode is an augmentation state in which a Vulcan can subcompute a thousand options before you can consider two. My logic-alternative mode can play the options out, many moves deep, in subtle detail, while taking in additional data—calculate with it to any number of decimals, make vital decisions—while still carrying on a conversation with Humans and a simultaneous confrontation with an enemy commander. But that Vulcan command mode, once engaged, cannot be switched off. Nor is it safely balked. A commander in that mode requires instant, unqualified, and detailed obedience. Those who cannot have followed his thought process must follow his orders—exactly. He

---

* "Star Trek" episode entitled "Errand of Mercy"; and "Mind-sifter" by Shirley Maiewski, from *Star Trek: The New Voyages*, No. 1, edited by S. Marshak and M. Culbreath

is obliged to give no explanation. I offer none. For your information, I am in Vulcan command mode and will so remain. You will conform to that fact."

Kirk raised a hand. "Question, sir?" he said quietly.

"One."

"Does a Vulcan in command mode ever give up—or ever make a mistake?"

For a long moment he thought that Spock *would* come through the desk. The "give up" was dirty pool. Spock had never suggested giving up again since Kirk's early, out-gunned Corbomite bluff succeeded.* Indeed, they had often bucked odds together that Spock calculated at thousands to one—against them. The "mistake" was possibly worse. Spock had made a few beauties—especially once or twice in early days when he had been in command, doubtless not using the full Vulcan mode, but being Vulcan enough to raise the hackles on stiff-necked Humans. Then Spock had gotten the hang of commanding Humans —extremely well.

But this Spock who had returned from Vulcan after all but succeeding in extirpating his Human half was not the same Spock.

He stood now with controlled deliberation, the cold, Kolinahr face turned on Kirk. "Mr. Kirk, that question is no longer yours to ask. You have no oath, no word, no honor even to abide by your own consent to serve under my command. You have risked your life, mine, Savaj's, the ship, the crew, and this mission—perhaps including the fate of the galaxy. You are self-confessed to insubordination and mutiny. You are unrepentant. You *are* unrepentant?"

Kirk weighed the answer for a long moment. "I regret that I was unable to obey your order. It is true I gave my oath to Starfleet discipline and my consent for you to take command. I broke that discipline and that word, risked all you have said. But *I* am not Vulcan. As what I am, I could do nothing else."

"Unrepentant," Savaj said, "and defiant. No fleet can exist without discipline."

Kirk shook his head. "No fleet can exist without disci-

---

* "Star Trek" episode entitled "The Corbomite Maneuver."

pline, and no sane sentient being can exist without 'some things which are beyond the discipline of the service.' "

That quote was still dirtier pool. "Beyond the discipline of the service" was the phrase Spock had used to Kirk about the secret of Vulcan "biology" that Spock would have died to keep. Spock very nearly *had* died when the *pon farr*, the deadly Vulcan time of mating, had hit him at a time when Starfleet ordered the *Enterprise* away from Vulcan—not knowing that the order was a death sentence for Spock. Kirk had broken the Vulcan's silence and a Starfleet Command order—to save Spock's life.* But the phrase had since become true of some of Spock's own command decisions.

"Captain Spock," Kirk said, "you also broke a direct Starfleet order—and violated the planet Gideon's strict 'keep out' order to search for me.** You gambled the Galileo Seven on a 'hunch' about my behavior.† Correctly. You risked galactic war with the Tholians rather than abandon one man who was considered dead—me—when I was trapped in the spatial interphase in the Tholian sector.†† It was not 'logical.' "

"You will *cease*," Spock thundered. After a moment he said icily, "You are relieved of status. You will not be seen or heard. You are confined to quarters, under guard."

Kirk felt his jaw set. Relieved of duty, authority—now not trusted even to confine himself to quarters.

"Sir," he said. "Request triple bridge or engineering duty in any capacity in lieu of inactive confinement as punishment."

"Denied. Confinement is *not* your punishment. You will be confined while I *consider* your punishment—according to the applicable Vulcan code."

Kirk stared at him. Indefinite suspension and confinement was bad enough. Full Starfleet trial would cost him his career, or worse. But everything he had seen of the planet Vulcan, from the Headsman in the Vulcan arena of marriage-and-challenge who punished cowardice to the casual disposal of the fate of Spock's betrothed wife,

* "Star Trek" episode entitled "Amok Time."
** "Star Trek" episode entitled "Mark of Gideon."
† "Star Trek" episode entitled "Galileo Seven."
†† "Star Trek" episode entitled "The Tholian Web."

T'Pring—whom he gave as property to Stonn*—to a few other things Kirk had learned over the years, suggested that a Vulcan's idea of a punishment to fit this crime would be intolerable.

It came home to Kirk now that in full Vulcan mode Spock would not find a way to let him off the hook.

"I ask pardon," Kirk said in what he hoped was a Vulcan manner.

Spock merely lifted an eyebrow. "Denied. Dismissed." He raised his voice. "Guard!"

The security guards came in.

After a moment Kirk turned with military precision and moved out of the pulsing red hell, not looking back at the Vulcans who had become his particular demons.

---

* "Star Trek" episode entitled "Amok Time."

Chapter Twelve

Spock sat down in the command seat and consulted the instruments on its arm controls, punched in the circuits that would give him remote access to most of his own science station's capabilities.

Savaj was working there now, playing it almost as Spock would have himself. The person who was missing from the bridge Spock did not consider.

Suddenly high voltage crackled around Spock's hands and froze them to the seat arm controls, convulsing his body so that he could not let go. Smoke rose from his hands.

He set his teeth against the agony and reached for the mental disciplines that might possibly override the body's overload. Break free— The effort was not working.

Dimly Spock saw Uhura and Sulu moving. "Cutting power," Chekov shouted, but the power did not cut.

Suddenly Savaj was there with a crushing double-handed smash to the seat controls, striking and pulling back with such power and speed that he did not become caught. Still the electricity crackled, spraying sparks now. Then Savaj's hand caught Spock and the sputtering voltage locked them together. But the power of Savaj's move hauled Spock out of the seat and they crashed together to the floor, breaking the connection.

"McCoy to bridge," Uhura called. "Mr. Spock has had an accident. I think—he's dead."

"It was no accident," Savaj said through his teeth.

Spock blanked out on the image of Savaj's face announcing Spock's murder.

McCoy saw Kirk burst into Sick Bay. Medical priority alert had sounded. The intercom had announced Spock's death, and Kirk's guard must either have yielded to his urgency or been tapped out by a Kirk who would not be stopped. Savaj had met McCoy at the turbolift, carrying Spock on the run. Spock was unconscious on the table, his hands a mass of burns. Readouts showed a flat graph on the heart line—complete heart failure caused by severe electrical shock.

McCoy was bending over Spock's abdomen with the paddles that might shock the Vulcan heart to revival. "Clear!" he snapped, and convulsed the Vulcan's body with the shock.

Nothing.

"Clear!" Again.

A faint bleep. A wavering climb of a display line, erratic, feeble. A beat. Then a sudden series of rapid beats. Finally the fast Vulcan heart rate caught in an irregular rhythm —faint, erratic, but *there*.

McCoy nodded fractionally, cautiously, to Kirk and continued to work on stabilizing Spock.

Kirk moved in with a hand on Spock's shoulder, impaled Savaj with a look, and snapped in the command tone, "What happened? Report."

"Murder," Savaj said.

McCoy's head jerked up from checking the heartbeat. Christine Chapel faltered in spray-dressing the hands.

"Electrical short?" McCoy growled. "How does that make it murder?"

"The command seat—" Savaj began.

"—has every electrical cutout in the book," Kirk finished.

"Precisely," Savaj said, "To divert sufficient power and to computer-suppress vital cutouts would have required

96

extremely sophisticated programming by an expert. Someone high in your crew, Doctor, is a murderer."

"Not if I can help it," McCoy swore. The Vulcan was still hanging on the edge, but it wasn't the first time they had pulled him back.

"Murder was intended," Savaj said. "All normal attempts to cut power failed. Human strength would not have sufficed to break the contact by main force. Had I not been on the bridge, murder would have been done."

"Thank you, Admiral," Kirk said.

Savaj did not answer him.

"That much power should have caught you, too, Admiral," McCoy said. "Wasn't that, by your standards, an illogical risk, too?"

"No, Doctor, a calculated risk and for commensurate gain. Nor was I caught. However—someone *was*."

He looked at Kirk.

"What?" McCoy said.

"The level of computer tampering would be possible only to Mr. Scott, Spock, myself—or Mr. Kirk."

"There is no one on that list," McCoy said carefully, "who has not loved Spock for years." He did not say, "Except—"

"Except myself," Savaj completed. "For all you do or can know. I believe you have established for the record that a Vulcan can kill for sufficiently logical reason."*

"Your scientific reputation is for saving lives," McCoy granted. "But we've believed reputations before. They are no guarantees against imposters, aliens—or even changed men. *V'Kreeth* Savaj, what says it couldn't be you?"

"Nothing, Doctor. Quite correct."

Kirk stepped forward. "Bones, I ran an identity check from the transporter pattern. He *is* Savaj of Vulcan." Then, remembering the power they must be up against, he added, "So far as our instruments can tell us."

McCoy sighed. "Well, I can't say I really doubted it. But *you* damn sure didn't try to kill Spock, Jim. Scott didn't."

"None of us could have, Bones. But someone tried."

Spock was breathing normally now, the heart pattern almost stable. That tough Vulcan psychosoma was fighting back.

McCoy nodded to Kirk. "Someone failed."

---

* "Star Trek" episode entitled "Journey to Babel."

"Let him rest," Kirk said. "Admiral Savaj, I am assuming command of this ship. I do not doubt you, but you are the stranger here, under conditions of alien assault involving capabilities we do not know. Murder is loose on my ship. It is still *my* ship. If you wish to bring charges against me under the discipline of the service, that is your privilege—later. Meanwhile command succession reverts to me in the absence of proven unfitness. You will now divulge all you know about this mission."

"No," Savaj said. "I will not. I do have the authority to replace you. My immediate concern, however, is that your status as chief suspect has now approached a probability of one. Certainty."

"Certainty?" Kirk said. "Hardly. There is, as the Doctor has pointed out, at least one alternative. Yourself. I do not suggest that. But some alien effect—"

"—could be operating through *you*, Mr. Kirk. Mr. Scott was not exposed to the aliens. Nor was I. Mr. Scott has been in full public view at critical times, while you have not. Mr. Spock has twice been a victim of attacks of unquestionably lethal potential. As have I, once. That leaves you. You have twice been exposed to alien mind-altering. More—you have been severely dealt with by your former First Officer and can expect much worse, if he lives."

"Admiral," Kirk said tightly. "I will consider some possibility of alien mind effect, even in myself, because I must. If you suggest that I myself have motive to murder Spock, I will cease to listen to illogic, sir."

"That part of your mind that could have motive would not be logical. Nor conscious. Nor under your control. I can suggest two unconscious motives of sufficient strength. It is a matter of record that your deepest fear is of losing command."*

Kirk looked at him sharply. "You know that record extremely well, sir." He shook his head. "I have *lost* command—once for nearly three years. I didn't go berserk."

"Didn't you?" Savaj said. "What do you consider the performance by which you got the *Enterprise* back?"**

* "Star Trek" episode entitled "And the Children Shall Lead."
** *Star Trek—The Motion Picture , A Novel*, by Gene Roddenberry

98

Kirk met his eyes. "Necessary. And—not murder. Name the other 'motive.' "

"It is related. You were part of a command team and a friendship that had become a legend in the service and on both your worlds. It was broken, not by your choice, when Spock brought his divided self home to Vulcan."*

Kirk looked at Savaj bleakly. "I will not deny what even a full Vulcan would suspect a Human might feel about that. But it would not make me a murderer."

"Not even when I came to put you under his command?" Savaj said. He stepped to the computer console, played in a program question.

"I have specified parameters of computer alteration skill, time, logistics, motive, opportunity, alien effect," Savaj spoke to the computer. "Computer, given those parameters, who on board *Enterprise* could be responsible for the attempts on Mr. Spock's life—and possibly also my own?"

"Working," the computer said. "Considering all parameters specified, only one suspect aboard—James T. Kirk."

Savaj turned to Kirk. "By that account, the *Enterprise* is commanded by a murderer."

---

* *Star Trek—The Motion Picture, A Novel*, by Gene Roddenberry

Chapter Thirteen

Kirk said, "Computer off." It hesitated an instant, consulting its basic programming against its recent conclusion. Finally it switched off.

Kirk faced Savaj. "Admiral, I do not know what is happening on this ship, but I *will* stop it. I no longer know whether you are part of the solution—or of the problem. I can conceive, even, that some alien mind-control technique might force me, or you, to murder. I will give such a technique no further opportunity."

"And if I order you as the ranking Starfleet Admiral to yield command?"

Kirk shook his head deliberately. "I yielded when it was not a matter of Spock's life or the ship's. Now it *is*— and I will not. I am and have been since you came aboard a commander in the field facing possible alien attack through imposture or mind alteration. Such a commander is not obliged to yield to what appears to be legitimate authority. I could yield to Spock. Alien effect or not, he is a part of that rapport which is unique to this command crew. In the end, I realize now, I will trust that rapport beyond anything else in the galaxy. Including, with all respect, you, sir."

"Fascinating," Savaj said. "However, it arrives at an

impasse. I also cannot permit alien influence—or murder
—to command."

"That will not be necessary."

It was Spock's voice, and Kirk whirled to see Spock still
immersed in that Vulcan healing state from which he
could nonetheless follow what was happening.

Savaj stepped over and slapped Spock, making Kirk
wonder how mere Human slaps had ever managed to
rouse Spock all these years. It was the only known way
to bring a Vulcan out of the healing trance, but it usually
took a Human a few hard slaps to make a Vulcan take
any notice.

The full Vulcan needed only one. Spock's eyes snapped
into focus, shaken. "That will do," he said, and moved to
sit up.

"You stay put, Spock," McCoy snapped. "Even you
can't walk away from the fact that five minutes ago you
were a dead man."

Spock stood up. He moved with great care to the computer. "Computer, specify alternative suspect."

"No viable alternative," the computer said.

"Spock," McCoy protested, "the computer has been
wrong before, including about Jim. You can't *believe*
that?"

Spock looked at McCoy levelly. "Suppose, Doctor, that
you wished through mind alteration to make a man capable
of murder. How would you do it?"

McCoy shrugged. "Hypnosis and other standard techniques, as a general rule, can't make a person violate a
deep moral code. However, they might change a person's
perception—make the subject believe the victim was
an attacker, an animal, a tree, a Jack the Ripper. Or they
might play on deep unconscious fears, hates, loves—buried
levels of emotion where the subject might believe the
victim deserved death."

"That was what *S'haile* Savaj described, Doctor. About
Kirk."

For a moment McCoy looked stopped, then he shook
his head. "Jim said he would stand on our rapport against
anything in the galaxy." McCoy stepped to Kirk's side.
"That goes for me, too."

After a moment he added, "Spock?"

Spock turned to Kirk. "What I believe has no logical

bearing on the question of whether your mind has been affected."

"And if it *has?*"

"Then, Mr. Kirk," Spock said, "it is quite possible that you are attempting to murder me."

Kirk stood very straight. After a moment Spock turned without a word and left Sick Bay.

Chaper Fourteen

Kirk came onto the bridge. Everyone except Captain Spock turned to look at him. Mr. Dobius escorted him, on orders from Spock not to let Kirk out of his sight.

Word had run through the ship like fire. Kirk knew it. They all knew it. Savaj had accused him of murder. And Spock, if he did not believe it, had at least not defended him.

Or—*did* Spock believe it? And was it, in some vestibule of hell, even *true*?

Kirk had gone round and round with that one. He was morally certain that he was not guilty of attempting murder—not on any level or for any reason. Certainly not of Spock. However, he had to face the fact that if he *were* guilty, he would be equally certain of his innocence. If the alien effect could force him to attempt murder, it could make him forget that he had done it.

"Commander Kirk reporting as ordered, Captain," he said. He saw looks of sympathy around the bridge, worry. Uhura, Sulu, Chekov. Were there any doubts?

Spock turned briefly in acknowledgment. "You may assume your post, Mr. Kirk. You remain under close arrest, subject to further punishment. Mr. Dobius, you will remain close at hand."

Spock turned back and Dobius stood stolidly as Kirk slipped into the science seat. At least, whatever Spock believed, he had brought Kirk out of quarters. To keep an eye on him? The better to consider what punishment was suitable—not only for saving Spock's life, but for killing him?

Kirk wanted to brood. But he wanted even more to figure out what had happened, stop it before it happened again. He ran every kind of computer search he could think of. It kept coming up with his name.

Kirk himself kept coming up with it. He alone knew just how badly he had been turned inside out and upside down at some deep level by the two encounters with the aliens. The guilt, the shame, the rage were still there, multiplied a hundredfold now, sitting just beneath the surface and threatening to engulf what was left of his sanity.

Savaj might be absolutely right. It was given to few men, perhaps to no man, to have a friendship such as he had had with Spock. He had never dealt with Spock's return to Vulcan except by some agreement with himself not to deal with it to its root.

Now, what if some skilled alien psychologist had gotten to that root?

Or what if the drive to command went even deeper than he knew? Or some combination, possibly even something much more simple and elemental—some unalterable programming to kill having little to do with him, but driving him?

If any of that were true, how would he prevent himself from killing Spock?

Kirk stood up. "Permission to leave the bridge, sir?"

"For what purpose?"

"Personal."

"Granted. Mr. Dobius, he will not be out of your sight."

"Yes, Captain."

Kirk considered the problem of Mr. Dobius. The Tanian was over seven feet tall, nearly half again as broad at the shoulders as Kirk, and in excellent training —all of which Spock had doubtless considered. With the Vulcan *asumi* training, even at his green sash level, a determined Kirk would not have had much trouble with almost any other non-Vulcan on the ship.

Kirk stopped outside security Sick Bay. "Mr. Dobius, you brought that prisoner back for me on my order. I consider that makes it our baby. You were present when Spock and Admiral Savaj tried to interrogate it?"

"Yes, sir."

"What did they learn?"

"Forgive me, sir," Dobius said quietly. "I am not certain of the ethics of this situation."

Kirk grinned. "That makes two of us, Mr. Dobius. However, if Admiral Savaj is right and I have been turned into a murderer—or a murder weapon aimed at Captain Spock, and perhaps Savaj or others also—then my basic alternative is to go jump over a cliff—or else to crack the problem. You presumably would attempt to stop me from the first. I submit the best way is to help me with the second."

Dobius looked at him carefully. "By letting you interrogate the prisoner?"

"An excellent suggestion, Mr. Dobius."

Dobius finally inclined his bifurcated head. "Sir, this ship has never recognized any division between you and Mr.—Captain Spock. I have had no orders not to discuss anything with you, nor to prevent you from acting as First Officer and Science Officer. But I must be with you."

"Thank you, Mr. Dobius." Kirk was through the force door before the words died.

The thing was still ugly and unnerving, and he hated it on sight. But now it was the prisoner, and it was alone. It stood near the far corner and looked at them with no expression they could read.

"Captain Spock and Admiral Savaj learned almost nothing," Dobius said. "It is alive, not a mechanism, probably communicates by some nonverbal means, but appears to have no telepathy and no empathy. It has effective mental shields and will not permit itself to be read. It may understand what we say via universal translator, but has not responded."

Kirk switched on the main security cell universal translator.

"I have been your prisoner. Now you are mine."

The no-mouth looked at him and backed a fraction

nearer to the corner, away from the diagnostic couch. Perhaps it read the rage in Kirk which would have liked to turn the tables on it—or to strap it to the tables. Perhaps it judged Kirk by itself and suddenly feared that he would do it.

Kirk nodded. "Yes. If I were *you*, I would have you strapped down there now, screaming—or whatever you do when you have to scream." He moved toward it menacingly. "Let's see what you do—"

There was some involuntary flicker and Kirk caught a glimpse of red behind a nictitating membrane on the no-mouth's domed forehead.

The universal translator read the visual pattern and emitted almost a cry.

"So you *do* scream," Kirk said. "So does a rose, you know. Or don't you know? Is it possible you don't know the pain you cause?"

The membrane flickered to show blue turning to coruscations of green. "Small lives"—the translator felt its way—"needed."

The membrane flashed up and this time it was a picture. The no-mouth with other no-mouths, two of them small, and some other life form, which the no-mouth held in its claw-arms with every appearance of affection. The picture dissolved to abstract color. "It is my task. . . . I serve. . . . I take no pleasure in rose scream. . . . I care for small lives of my own."

"Every concentration camp guard could say the same," Kirk said coldly, "and did. Everybody who ever carved up a living being had some pet dog or small life of his own. Whom do you serve?"

"We serve. We do task. We report. We are not to know how each task serves. It would spoil the study."

"Who is making the study?"

The no-mouth almost shrugged, despite lacking the anatomy for it. "*They* study. We serve. You—perform. At need, you die."

"Not anymore," Kirk said. "You will tell me how to reach these studiers. Or *I* will do the serving, and *you* can try the dying."

The picture of no-mouths at home flashed again.

"Not interested," Kirk said. "*Your* small lives are needed for *my* purposes, now."

The no-mouth backed away hard against the corner. Kirk motioned Dobius forward.

The no-mouth flashed a star map, identifiable after a moment as the Helvan system—then Helvan, a planet map, main city, the alien installation, then a tortuous trail through energy field canyons to the lone mountain that rose above the city.

For a moment Kirk caught a glimpse of a great ship descending down into the crater of the ancient volcano, then a shimmering glimpse as of alien forms indistinctly seen—perhaps humanoid. Perhaps the no-mouths did not care to look at them too closely.

"Show me again," Kirk said. "The path."

This time he cut in a Vulcan trick of concentration Spock had once tried to teach him and engraved the trail on his memory. But he still could get no clearer picture of the enemy at trail's end.

At least he knew that there was someone beyond these no-mouths. He felt no consuming hate for them now—merely contempt and a dull loathing. Now it was the ones beyond, the planners, whom he wanted to wipe off the face of the galaxy.

"Do not—serve—me?" the no-mouth flickered.

Kirk resisted the impulse to tell it that he had never intended to. They might need to question it again. And it could suffer at least the anticipation, for what it and its kind had done to him and his.

"Not just this minute," he told it. "If you continue to cooperate perhaps I will choose you for some service you would survive." He looked at it for a moment, picturing it and its kind in all their millions or billions, and all their work, perhaps for centuries or millennia.

What they had done to him, multiplied and compounded, was all represented by this small civil servant of evil.

He went out and made it to his quarters before he was violently sick.

Chapter Fifteen

There was a knock at the door, peremptory and summoning, ignoring the usual signal.

Kirk pulled himself together, flashed a look at Mr. Dobius, and went to face the music.

"Come."

The music was Vulcan, a duet for two thunderclouds—Spock, Savaj. Somehow McCoy had managed to turn up too. They came into Kirk's quarters.

"Mr. Kirk," Spock said, "you have left your post on personal privilege and used that excuse to interrogate the prisoner without consent or consultation with your commanding officer."

Kirk drew himself up. "I said my reason was personal. It was. I take what the prisoner's kind did to me very personally. And it is I, personally, if Admiral Savaj is right, who will kill you, unless we solve this problem. Before that, I would do a great deal more than interrogate without consultation—which is my right since you returned me to duty."

Spock shook his head. "We established that for any dangerous procedure involving alien effects you would have me present for protection. I will add this to my consideration in weighing consequences."

"I had Mr. Dobius," Kirk said.

Spock flashed Dobius a look that should have withered him like grass. "So I see."

"Those *were* my only orders, sir," Dobius said.

Spock nodded. "In future I will specify." He dismissed it and turned back to Kirk. "Report."

"The prisoner is—only what we would call a lab technician. A junior league experimenter who injects the experimental animal with cancer. It . . . loves its little no-mouths and its pet puppy and is quite willing to use our small lives for its higher purposes. It only follows orders. It does not care what pain it causes. It 'has its task.' It merely 'serves—'" Kirk stopped himself. The arguments had been made before—by members of his own species. The arguments did not make the no-mouth, or Kirk's own species, less guilty, but the worst guilt was elsewhere. "This alien is not who, or what, we have to find."

"The Designers," Savaj said.

They turned to him. "There has always, necessarily, been someone or something beyond these experimenters," Savaj said. "The essence of the double-blind experimental design is that neither the subjects nor the experimenters shall know who is in the experimental group and who are the controls. It is the only scientific design that defeats the illogical susceptibility of intelligent beings to placebo effects and terminal self-delusion."

"Even Vulcans?" McCoy asked.

Savaj did not look pleased. "Logic protects. It does not obliterate the design of the mechanism. Humans attempted to eliminate placebo effects. Vulcans made them the basis of medicine. Both solutions still require the double-blind. The necessity, however, is not of much consolation to the control subject who dies while the experimental group receives the real cure for cancer. Nor to those killed by false cures. The price of knowledge has always come high."

"Then . . . *we* are the subjects," Kirk said.

"Or the controls," McCoy added.

"Both," Savaj said. "And such experimenters as we have reached are as blind as we about which worlds serve what purpose. The grand design is elsewhere and the Designers—yet unknown."

"Perhaps not," Spock said. "Mr. Kirk, how were you able to obtain this knowledge from the 'experimenter'?"

Kirk smiled fractionally. "I'm afraid I conveyed to him the impression that the rat was about to turn the tables on him."

"Bluff," Spock said.

Kirk nodded. "It worked—because *he* would have done it."

Spock looked at him with interest. "I believe you have said something, Mr. Kirk. The Designers also must have some blind spot. Callousness is always blind. There must be something we could use. A third blind . . ."

"Spock!" Kirk said. "You've hit it! Gentlemen, do you remember the story of the rats who trained the psychologists . . . ?"

In the end it was settled. Spock would never know that Kirk had given some thought to going off and tackling it alone, as Spock had against Vejur. Apart from serving the Vulcan right, it would at least have removed Spock from the threat of being murdered by Kirk.

However, he had possibly pushed his luck with Spock once too often. Nor was there much of a snowball's chance on Helvan that he would even get through alone to learn something, let alone get back to report it.

"Suppose," he said finally, "that we try to attract enough attention to get picked up out of the maze?"

"To do *what?*" McCoy said. "Argue? Get dissected? Animals who attract too much attention in my laboratory experience don't fare too well."

"I know, Bones. I'm asking us to use ourselves as bait for beings about whom we know nothing, except that they are incredibly powerful and that they are willing to pay the price for knowledge—in other living beings' lives."

For a long moment they stood silent, perhaps even the Vulcans contemplating that that was the heart of terror.

Finally Spock said, "We will go. Savaj and I."

Kirk shook his head. "*I* am the one who knows the route. It is a visual impression that I tried to capture by Vulcan mnemonics, but which I will have to feel out as I go. I'm not certain that I *could* communicate it, even by mind-link. But even if I could, I am not willing, and you would not force it. I'm going."

"Mr. Dobius was also present and is better equipped for planetary hazards."

"With all due respect, sir," Dobius said, "I do volunteer, but we cannot be certain that what I saw is the same as what Mr. Kirk saw—nor that I can reconstruct it."

"Spock," Kirk said, "we *must* go. I have a hunch that whoever is staging this may have some interest in one or more of us, or our particular combination. Something has been at pains either to make me attempt to murder you or to make it appear that I have done so. The only possible alternative is Admiral Savaj—or direct action by some method unknown. I can't let you go alone with Savaj. And if someone has gone to the trouble to test us against suspicion, doubt, murder—maybe they'll want to continue the test, pick us up—"

"Jim's right," McCoy said. "The test is *us*. I'll get my medical kit."

"You do not imagine that *you* are going, Doctor?"

"Spock, no hazard party will now leave this ship without its Chief Medical Officer while I hold that position."

For a moment Kirk had seen the look in Spock's eyes of the Vulcan command mode, considering and discarding options. The mode was harsh, but ruthlessly logical even against the Vulcan's own strong resistance.

"You are saying: The Designers may be studying, among other things, our rapport." He nodded. "I yield to that point. Landing party will consist of myself, Savaj, Kirk, and Dr. McCoy."

They gathered equipment and beamed down to the camouflaged opening of the force-shielded canyon that, according to the no-mouth, led to the only opening it knew to the Designer complex under the great mountain.

Kirk closed his eyes and tried to recall the appropriate visual. He opened them and walked to the concealed opening, found it.

Spock led the way through into a staggering interlocking series of canyons, the sheer mirrored cliffs a thousand feet high and looking the same in all directions.

"I wish," McCoy said plaintively, "that you hadn't called it a *maze*."

* * *

Spock moved off in silence, as if he barely tolerated Kirk's presence, not speaking unless to give a curt order. Now and then McCoy attempted some normal grouse or grumble, trying to lighten the atmosphere. Once Kirk followed up with some normal rejoinder. It was met with such glacial silence by the two Vulcans, especially Spock, that Kirk subsided and for once was quiet and very thoughtful.

There was no getting around the fact that he had really done it this time. With some attempt at fairness he tried to put himself in Captain Spock's position. What if Kirk's First Officer had gone against his direct and binding orders, barging in on his carefully laid plan—even if that plan included a high probability of his death, risking ship and mission in plain mutiny, and, after being placed under threat of full punishment, possibly making an attempt on his life? Possibly worse than *that*—pulling an unauthorized and dangerous breach of authority again in questioning the alien.

If Spock had released him now for essential duty, the Vulcan was still making it plain that Kirk would yet have to answer to him.

Chapter Sixteen

Sunset painted the glittering thousand-foot crystal cliffs with flame. It would have been one of the most spectacular tourist attractions of the galaxy, hell on Helvan, mirroring itself in incandescent sheets of flame, skyscraper-high and reflecting each other like the endless corridors of a hall of mirrors.

It was breathtaking, also blinding—and hotter than the hinges of Hades, as McCoy was heard to complain.

It was also totally confusing. Kirk's mental pictures made no sense in that flame-on-flame inferno. He believed he had picked the right central canyon when they started. He hoped they had not come to the first crucial turning. Beyond that he could not say. The bottom of the canyon was filled with shattered crystal, like a fall of diamonds, through which great black and silver trees grew. Now and then one grew on some ledge on a cliff face, looking like a Japanese painting done on a flaming mirror.

Kirk and McCoy were laboring in the heat, the heavy gravity. The gravity difference had been merely a background nuisance—until they started to climb in it. Now it was a slow drain on the two Humans. For the Vulcans it was a refreshing gambol. Did Vulcans gambol? Actually they climbed with that ease by which they did not even

117

notice the effort, now and then giving a hand or a boost to a Human.

Then, almost as if a switch had been turned off, the sun dropped with finality behind the thousand-foot cliffs and darkness fell. In the last rays of the light horned demons jumped out at them and heaved deadly six-foot shards of crystal at them.

Spock and Savaj closed in front of Kirk and McCoy and blocked some of the mirror-spear barrage with field packs, knocked some of it aside with *asumi* moves. The attackers, Kirk saw, must be back-of-beyond Helvans, still in the Stone Age.

"Back," Spock ordered, and the party retreated up a cliff path. Spock would be reluctant to use phasers, although the planet was already heavily contaminated with interference from the experimenters and the Designers.

They reached a turn where a large crystal overhang reached out over the path. Spock and Savaj traded a look and put their shoulders to the massive overhang. They heaved together and the overhang sheared off at its top and went careening down the sloping path, scattering attackers, who leaped out of its way.

When the crystal dust settled, the attackers appeared to have lost nerve. They huddled at the bottom of the path, then moved off.

That was virtually the last thing the Humans of the *Enterprise* party could see. The night became black as a pocket.

Kirk sensed rather than saw Spock move off up the cliff path, surefooted as some cross between mountain goat and cat. Kirk felt a hand on his elbow. Savaj steered him up the path, stopped to collect McCoy.

They found Spock exploring a large crystal cave. The interior was faintly luminescent. Great sheets of mirroring crystal stood at angles here too, turning their foursome into serried ranks of Vulcans and Humans.

"I assume your mental pictures will not function in darkness, Mr. Kirk. Nor is it prudent to move in the dark while under attack—or with Humans who lack night vision. We will stay here." Spock and all his myriad mirror images moved off into the back of the cave.

They broke out camping gear, put up the force field equivalent of a thorn-boma in the mouth of the cave—it would also block light from their fire and dissipate smoke. Savaj hauled in a dead silver tree from somewhere before they closed it. He carried it like a branch on his shoulder. It had looked like a ming tree from a distance, but the size suggested it had aspirations to be a redwood. Savaj carried it easily and snapped off some branches with his hands to start the fire. Spock finally returned with an armload of something that looked rather like blue mushrooms. Kirk saw him analyze them to the last alkaloid with the tricorder, nod satisfaction, and toast them on sticks over Savaj's fire. Kirk sensed that some primordial sense of battles shared and safely won around a warriors' campfire had even reached the Vulcans. The offenses were not forgotten, but the glacial atmosphere had thawed slightly. Kirk broke out coffee and McCoy fussed over a couple of cuts Kirk had caught on an arm in the brief encounter with the natives.

Presently they were sitting down to what proved to be surprisingly delicious roasted blue mushrooms, hot coffee, and a momentary, if false, sense of safety. Kirk remained acutely aware of the literal and figurative maze they were in—the trapped, helpless sense of the rat whose bold move to master his fate would lead him, at best, into the heart of hell. Still, there were worse ways to arrive at that destination than to have a moment over this fire, with friends.

"You know," McCoy said, "I could get used to having a couple of Vulcans around the camp."

Kirk chuckled. "I second the motion, Bones. You and I would be having canned rations, canned heat, and cold comfort—assuming our bones weren't stretched out somewhere down the path."

Savaj looked mildly surprised, as if he could not for a moment place what the Humans were talking about. "Nothing unusual has happened," the full Vulcan said.

Kirk chuckled. "No, of course not, Admiral. Nothing unusual. But unless I miss my guess, sir, you also have enjoyed that 'nothing unusual.' We Humans are something of a trial for you, but we call forth your natural capacities in ways that must be satisfying. You *have* enjoyed it, *V'Kreeth* Savaj?"

Savaj appeared to consult some inner calculator. "I would not designate the state as an emotion, but there is a certain pleasurable release of capacity." He lowered a frown on Kirk's smile. "As well as severe and frequent irritation."

Kirk stretched out on an elbow on one of the force-down sleeping bags. "I don't doubt it. You know, the gulf between Vulcan and Human is very narrow, but . . . it is very deep." He looked at Spock. "I know you, Spock, as I know no one else in the galaxy, and half of you is flesh of my flesh, kind of my kind, as Human as I am. And yet somewhere at the bottom of that gulf remains a mystery. The Designers." He looked at Savaj. "What if the gulf between us and them really *is* the gulf between rat and man?"

"That is the question I have lived with, Mr. Kirk—for ten years," Savaj said.

"When the psychologists were studying the rats, sir," Kirk said, "on my planet, or yours—was there anything they could have learned by interrogating the rat?"

Savaj looked at Kirk carefully. "It has been my whole aim and focus for those ten years, Commander, to communicate to the Designers that there *is*."

Kirk studied the Vulcan. "You have been trying to get picked up out of the cage from long before I suggested it, haven't you?"

"Much longer. Since I began to suspect what the Designers are studying."

"Which is?"

"The Promethean fault, Commander. The flaw in the design of intelligent life that may ultimately annihilate it, and us."

"You said," McCoy interposed, "that they were studying aggression."

Savaj nodded. "That is the flaw in the machine, Doctor. All intelligent corporeal life appears to retain aggression as an integral part of its makeup. Yet at some point intelligence necessarily develops the power to destroy itself and all it touches—without ever losing the aggression that once belonged to the unarmed animal."

McCoy nodded. "Nobody ever quite licked that one—not even Sargon's people.* They survived their early atomic crisis and maybe a million years beyond, seeded

---

* "Star Trek" episode entitled "Return to Tomorrow."

the galaxy with their offspring—maybe including us—and still destroyed each other by war. We've met . . . I don't know how many others. The five-hundred-year computer war— But maybe the answer is just the one Jim gave those people. Yes, we have the killer instincts, but 'we're not going to kill today.' "

Savaj nodded. "Admirable, Doctor. Vulcan gave that answer a thousand years ago. It has virtually ended the killing. It has not ended the problem. I translate it for you as the Promethean problem. Vulcan has a similar legend —as do most species. Mr. Spock would understand it in your terms."

Spock's face had an abstracted expression—not quite any look Kirk had ever seen—as if he were attuned to something not heard.

"Prometheus brought fire to man," Spock said, "and for his reward was chained to a rock to be eaten by vultures. What is disquieting is that intelligent life forms all over the galaxy understand that legend—both the fire-bringing and the vultures."

Spock stirred the fire with a stick, looked into the coals and up at Kirk. "There is both the god in man, which reaches for fire and stars, and that black-dark streak, which steals the fire to make chains, extracts a price from the fire-bringer, and lets loose the dogs of war and the vultures of destruction. There is the greatness—and the callousness."

His eyes examined Kirk as if he would read some riddle there. "Nor are we alone in that duality—your species or mine. Every solution to the Promethean flaw that intelligent corporeal life in the known galaxy has found is, at best, partial—It is also . . . temporary."

Spock looked up through the mouth of the crystal cave in the direction where the unseen alien mountain stood waiting for them.

"Nevertheless," Spock said, "it is *our* solution."

Kirk followed Spock's eyes up to where the silent mountain and the Designers' own final solution brooded over them. He found himself shivering. It was the chill of the night, he told himself, or the physical shocks of the day. But the weight of shame and terror closed down on him again, now with crushing force. The Promethean question was older than man. But if the Designers were still studying it at world's end, when they stood to him as man to rat, then what hope was there?

And what complaint would they want to hear from the rat?

He had put himself, his closest friends, and perhaps the last hope of intelligent life in this galaxy into the hands of Zeus. And the chains and the vultures were at hand.

Savaj of Vulcan reached over and programmed Kirk's force-down sleeping bag to close around him. "I will stand watch," Savaj said. "Whatever they have done to you, you need not fear what you will do tonight."

floor. McCoy was suddenly there, taking possession of the hurt hand.

"I—tried to kill you, Spock?" Kirk said.

"No," Spock said firmly. "Something that was done to you aimed you at me—and might merely have succeeded in making you go over the cliff. It is a test. We should have known that it was always a test."

He turned toward the mountain, barely visible in cold dawn light above the cliffs. "It has failed," he said, as if he spoke to someone not present. "I do not suspect him, and he is not yours to use. That which you do not understand is stronger than any wedge you have tried to drive between us. We, both and all, stand on that rapport against you."

He put a hand on Kirk's arm and on McCoy's and nodded to Savaj, who still retained a light hold on Kirk's shoulder. "Will you study *that*—to our faces?" Spock asked the mountain.

Kirk felt as if something flowed from the two Vulcans' touch to surround them with a protection, a unity. A line from a very old poem came to him. "And we, all we are against thee, oh God most high. . . ."

It was not God they challenged, but the temerity was of the same order of magnitude. "It is a terrible thing to fall into the hands of the living God. . . ." Or of the ultimate evil at world's end.

The crystal cliffs shimmered. Then Kirk knew that it was they who were dissolving in some unknown effect. Well, they had asked to be picked up. . . .

They emerged into a mirrored hall that would have accommodated God—or giants in the Earth. No, it was not mirrored, exactly. The walls were some form of in-depth hologram, where their images were projected in three dimensions and in an endlessly reflected, diminishing series that disappeared at infinity. The corridor itself stretched to some vanishing point of perspective.

It was compellingly beautiful—requiring a technology that could not have been matched in the known galaxy— and Kirk had the feeling that it was nothing more than an undecorated holding cage to the Designers.

Where were those Designers? And were they built on a scale to match these hundred-foot-high walls? Or would a hand reach down on a hundred-foot arm to lift him?

"Whose bright idea was *this?*" McCoy muttered, trying to take the edge off awe—or terror.

"Ours, Doctor," Spock said, leading off in a direction that seemed as good as any other. "It seems to have been adopted with some alacrity."

"Where *are* we?" McCoy asked. "In that mountain?"

"Possibly," Savaj said. "If we are on Helvan or in any ordinary dimension at all."

Kirk looked a question at him.

Savaj shrugged. "From the days of your planet's UFO phenomena their ships have not seemed to follow ordinary laws of physics. It is my hypothesis that they travel alternate dimensions of reality as easily as we travel to stars. We may be in an outpost on Helvan—or somewhere else entirely."

And, Kirk thought, in any case quite beyond the reach of the *Enterprise,* or any help at all.

"What concept would a rat have of being taken to a laboratory?" McCoy said.

Kirk turned to see that Leonard McCoy's face was gray. It finally came home to Kirk that he had not fully thought how this would look from a doctor's eye view. Much had been done toward the humane treatment of animals in medicine. And yet it was still sometimes McCoy's task to find out what made some small alien organism tick—perhaps to save the life of a man or of the ship. The doctor knew only too well that they were presenting themselves to be put under the microscope on slides.

Kirk moved closer to McCoy. There wasn't the hell of a lot more he could do. He could feel that his own face would be white around the eyes. "Cheer up, Bones. Maybe it's only psychologists."

McCoy nodded sourly. "Sure. That's why they had you strapped to that table."

Spock, investigating the hologram surfaces with his hands, found one where his hand went through. They gathered in front of a section that looked no different from the others, reflecting their solid images to infinity. But Spock gathered them behind him and stepped squarely into the Spock solid that came to meet him. It was as if both solid Spocks dissolved at some expanding surface line where they met. The line shimmered like a ripple of quicksilver.

"Come on!" Kirk said, and suddenly bolted forward into his own image beside the Vulcan, afraid that the thing would prove to be some dimension gate to elsewhere entirely and they would be separated. He still had a grip on McCoy's arm and he sensed that Savaj suddenly caught hold of McCoy from behind. It required an effort of logic to run smack into his own solid image, but he felt no impact, only an odd dissolving sensation that passed through him. He was into the plane of dissolution before Spock had quite disappeared.

Then Spock caught him and pulled them all through like beads on a string. But Kirk had the sinking feeling that if he had not moved before the mirror membrane closed, they would have been cut off.

He saw the same suspicion in Spock's eyes. "In future at any such juncture, maintain physical contact," Spock ordered.

Now they were in some Chamber that seemed to be made of hammered gold—including the space they had just stepped through, which now tested as solid wall. The chamber was small. The gold ceiling was well over three times their height.

They investigated every reachable inch of wall. Nothing. Kirk turned to find Savaj offering the stirrup of his hand. Kirk stepped into it, started to go to Savaj's shoulders—but the gold ceiling was much higher than that. Savaj lifted Kirk to the full stretch of his arms and he was still several feet short. Savaj lowered him a little, then heaved to give him a good toss as Kirk jumped. He was prepared to bounce off the ceiling, but he jumped as if his hands would go through it to catch the top of the wall. They did.

He pulled himself up to sit on the top of the wall, being careful not to go through the ceiling entirely. From the top it felt solid, but he could still lean down through it. Above there was a broad expanse of crystal gardens, apparently open air, and lavender sky—and the black and silver trees.

He bent down through the ceiling. "Come on up. Eden has arrived."

"I don't care if it's heaven," McCoy said. "I'm a doctor, not a gymnast."

In point of fact, it did not look easy. McCoy was pretty

active, but he was not in that kind of training. And somebody was going to have to be last man. Kirk doubted that even a Vulcan could catch a hand from a standing leap.

"Go on," McCoy said. "I can at least give a leg up. Leave me."

Kirk started to swing a leg back over.

Savaj paid no attention to either of them. He merely nodded to Spock. Spock did a running mount to the full Vulcan's hands, then was heaved up as he put his own momentum into a leap. Spock arrived beside Kirk, caught hold, and pulled himself up. Then he was managing some maneuver by which he braced with one leg and leaned down almost the full stretch of his body. From there he could catch McCoy's wrist from Savaj's lift. Spock pulled McCoy up as easily as he had caught Kirk with one hand at the top of his jump and lifted him up out of the dungeon where aliens from another galaxy had appeared to them as Sylvia and Korob. Spock lifted McCoy from a still greater height until Kirk caught him at the last and parked him on the wall. And Kirk still didn't think Savaj could make it.

He was wrong. He saw Savaj back off, gather full Vulcan mental focus, then make a deliberate running leap for Spock's hand. Kirk had read that some famous dancers of past or present—Nijinski, T'Vreel—seemed to leap higher and stay up longer than physics allowed. He had not seen it. Until now. Savaj seemed to reach the last inches more by levitation than anything else.

Spock caught him by fingertips. This time it was no joke for Spock to lift the full Vulcan's weight. Spock's muscles rippled and knotted and Kirk leaned down to try to brace him. Then Savaj was pulling himself up and gaining the wall, helping Spock back up after him.

Finally the ceiling closed behind them and they were catching their breath on a carpet of crystal with diamonds in their hair.

Kirk heard the sound of silvery laughter behind him. "Gentlemen," he said. "You may proceed. I, personally, have gone right off the deep end."

Chapter Eighteen

"You have," Spock said, looking over Kirk's shoulder, "company."

But whether he meant himself in the company of madness or the company of some presence approaching, Kirk was not certain. He turned, coming up on his knees, ready to make it to his feet and face anything.

Well, almost anything. He realized that he had been prepared for monsters, monstrosities, giants, gods, demons, the local equivalent of Organians, any of the life forms he had faced or not faced—or their million-year-later descendants.

He was not prepared for one perfectly ordinary humanoid female.

He came to his feet slowly. No, not ordinary. Not Human, either. But close enough that his old standards of beauty still applied, and any biochemistry he owned. She was tall, lithe, and exotic, smooth muscles shaping curves he could appreciate. She seemed to be wearing mainly an illusion that might have been silver feathers shimmering in a force field. But her ears also swept up to tips, which appeared almost winged—not Vulcan, but with an equal grace, and blending into spun silver that might have been hair, feathers, the actual metal—or all three.

Kirk could not make out what was her and what was artifice—nor did he care. He caught Spock's eye, the Vulcan's resigned look of observing a predictable reaction—a string of names stretching back nearly ten years—Sylvia, Deela, Kalinda, and all the others—and read Captain Spock's implied consent to go try the predictable gambit. Kirk moved toward her, tried his best smile, trusting to that common language, at least, and hoping for the best with his implant translator.

"Hello. Are you brought here as we are?"

She looked him over. "I am here."

Kirk chuckled. "I never doubted it for a moment." He sobered. "We are strangers here. Who belongs in this place?"

"You, henceforth."

He shook his head. "Not unless we are prisoners. We wish only to communicate with those who trouble our worlds. Do you know them?"

She made a slight movement of long-fingered hands. "So far as they are to be known."

He reached out to capture one of the hands and she allowed it. There was a faint sculpture of feathery silver at her wrist, but whether it was adornment or a vestige of nightingale, he could not tell. "I hope . . . you are not alone here," he said.

She withdrew the hand. "No, I am not."

"Do you have a name?"

"You may designate me Belen."

"Belen. It has the sound of silver bells."

He heard the silvery laughter again. "No. It does not."

"Are you a captive here?" he asked.

She stood contained now and merely looked at him. "No, little one, I am not."

He felt his eyes widen, but he knew that he had felt the shock creeping up on him for some time now. It made his legs not want to take his weight. He was seeing the no-mouths and their strap-down tables and this silver vision standing over them with her quicksilver laughter.

"You are the captor," he said.

"Why, no," she said from her cool containment. "You were never free."

"What *are* you, then?" he said harshly.

"I project the forthcoming," she said blandly. "At need

I select limited-purpose subjects, or perhaps gentle them for handling."

"And is that what you are doing now? Gentling?"

She made the hand gesture he now read as "Beyond your ken." "So far as it can be put in terms you would believe you understood."

"I understand," Kirk said, "that I and my people have been manipulated, mind-controlled, subjected to physical pain and mental abuse, pushed to the point of murder or suicide. Our worlds have been pushed to revolution, war, chaos, and impending destruction. We have been put in a maze and made to perform for your amusement or edification. And now you want to *gentle* us?"

"No, little one. I *have*. Your performance on the elementary problems was satisfactory. You show substantial communication and cohesiveness. You did not, quite, kill, although severely bound to do so. There was always some small margin for escape, if in nothing but the resistant physiology and known rescue proclivities of the two V subjects. In the end, your own resistance was . . . interesting. There appears to be a capacity for personal affinity bonds of rather surprising resistance to tampering, stress, and suspicion." She looked at him and there was some attentive expression in her silver-black eyes that seemed to read him on some level he had not intended to write. "Such a capacity might also be interesting."

Kirk gave her the counterpart of that look, with interest.

"Remind me to show you some time—if I can get past the fact that you set me to kill my friend. And—my Captain. Not to mention Admiral Savaj, whose record and person I would honor if I had to pick three names out of a galaxy."

The silver-black eyes darkened to black. "You will subside. Small life does not speak in a tone of reprimand."

Kirk stood his ground. "I wish no quarrel with you. I have come to tell you that my life is precious to me, as yours is to you. I feel pain as vividly. If a rose can scream, how much more a living, feeling, breathing, loving, intelligent being? I love. I choose my affinities and cherish them. I defend what is mine, my life, my friends, my worlds. Whatever you are, if you are able to do all of this, you are able to know my pain. I come to ask you to let me and mine go—all worlds of this galaxy where you touch and twist our lives."

The eyes flecked with silver again. "Little one, do you really suppose it would be so simple?"

"Do you suppose I could fail to ask?"

She spread her hands, acknowledging, shrugging. "When the pleading eyes have looked up at you from some cage, small one, begging you for their still smaller lives, have you stayed your hand?"

Kirk set his teeth. It was a sore point that had been rubbing something raw at the back of his mind since they had been plunged into the nightmare of being caged themselves. Their hands were not clean. His weren't. "No," he said. "Not always. But we try not to cause needless suffering. And we do not use the lives of intelligent life forms."

She looked at him with mild surprise. "Neither do we."

He found himself staring at her. "You don't believe we are intelligent? You studied us on a starship."

"The beavers of your world, small one, engineer lodges and dams. Your chimpanzees learn to use symbols as speech. Vulcan *snarth* and Terran dolphins have speech of their own. They feel. They love. They have been hunted, domesticated, trained, experimented on. And eaten. Do you never eat flesh, small one?"

"Most of that," Kirk said tightly, "has been centuries ago."

She crossed her hands. It looked like a gesture of negation. "A moment in time. Nor have you ended it entirely. We take no pleasure in your pain. We are quite familiar with your capacities. That they bear some marginal resemblance to our own is what makes you useful to us. But there is less distance between you and the analogy you have used—the rat—than between you and us. And, as was always your argument, and as it still is—our own lives are at stake."

"How?" Kirk said, but she was turning.

"Follow me, small one."

He hung back for a moment. "And if I don't?"

She turned back, the eyes as black as space, then glittering with some cold spark. He suddenly felt fire run along every nerve. He swayed, fighting it, trying not to cry out. Then he was on the ground. It stopped, but he

132

sensed something behind him. He turned to see McCoy collapsing, the two Vulcans locked into iron resistance and still not shaking it off.

"Stop it!" he snapped.

"Rephrase. Alter tone."

He took a breath. "Stop it, please."

She stopped and Spock moved to lift McCoy from the ground, held him while he tried to stand. Kirk made it to his feet under his own power. Just.

"Follow me." She did not say please. Nor did they argue.

Chapter Nineteen

Kirk fell back to where Spock and Savaj were helping McCoy, hopefully out of earshot or translator range of the Designer. Belen.

She was still shockingly beautiful, a sculpture in flesh and silver, now moving like a goddess ahead of them, and he felt nothing but a kind of cold horror. Nor did it help that some of that horror was at himself. This was the heritage of his species, too—the using of lives. And if they were better about it now than Neanderthal man or Genghis Khan or Colonel Green, they still had a ways to go. Nor did he have an answer that he would apply to all cases. But he knew his answer would not be the Designers' answer.

"Bones?" he said.

McCoy gritted his teeth. "I have a few left. I'm okay, Jim."

Kirk nodded, looked ruefully at Spock, indicating his failure with Belen "It's known as striking out, Captain Spock. Sorry " Spock merely nodded.

It was Savaj who answered.

"I believe the proper expression, Mr. Kirk, concerns the impossibility of emerging victorious in a totality of cases."

"You can't win 'em all," McCoy translated. "Of course, you've been known to try."

Kirk shot him a look that said, "Later for you," but he dropped his voice to say to Spock, "You or Savaj better take the next one, Spock. At least you are vegetarians." His voice sounded sour, even to him.

"One could wish the same could be said of the Designers," Spock said.

Kirk looked at him sharply. "You don't think that they—"

"Unknown. I think not. However, certain distinctions among different kinds of small lives may not be as clear to the Designers as we would prefer. Ethically, however, I do not suppose that it makes much difference to a small life for what purpose its life is used."

Kirk grimaced. "I suppose not." But the thought of what they might be used for stayed with him. Maybe it would make a difference?

Belen turned and stopped at a grove of silver trees. Kirk moved ahead, fast, not wanting McCoy to suffer for his sins. She was waiting, not patiently.

The silver tree grove picked itself up on its roots and divided to form an aisle, which ended in an impressive entrance The entrance was quite plain and functional. It merely appeared to have been poured out of a rainbow.

"Everything here," Kirk said to Belen. "appears to serve a purpose. while being exquisitely beautiful." He looked at her. still trying a little, he supposed, just to keep his hand in.

Her silver-feathery eye-winglines lifted. "How else would it be?" She gestured him through the door. He gave it up and moved past her. "*You* are permitted without alteration." she said behind him.

He turned quickly. but caught no look on her face but bland contemplation. He didn't think he wanted to answer for the look on his own face. Had she called him beautiful?

Then a thought struck a chill into him and he almost asked if she meant also the others could enter without—alteration. He bit it off, not to give her any ideas, and started to move on again, assuming it. But she stopped him and turned to look at the others. Was she reading his thoughts? He tried to stop thinking.

She raked her eyes over the others as if inspecting them properly for the first time. Savaj, Spock. But Kirk was not in much doubt how either of those would strike a female of almost any species. She moved to McCoy and tipped his chin up. McCoy met her eyes steadily, but he did not look well. "It needs care," she said.

"I will care for him," Spock said quickly.

She shrugged her hands. "See that it does not suffer, or I must attend to it."

She turned back to Kirk. "My friend," he said carefully, "is a skilled physician—a learned man and a natural healer. He is essential to me. To all of us."

"Let him heal himself," she said. "Sickness communicates. I cannot have sick small life. Apart from that, each will do, in his fashion. Come."

She led them through the door.

Spock had no difficulty as a scientist in discerning the pattern of a laboratory. Holocube displays were tuned in on experiments in progress on what appeared to be an indefinitely large number of worlds. The holocubes diminished into the distance to the vanishing point. Nearby ones showed some scenes Spock could place as to world. Helvan. Andor with its blue skin and white horn-antennae. Several pig-faced Tellarite worlds. The tiny winged dragons of Kar-lee. Rigel IV. Earth. Vulcan. The Romulan heartworlds. The interior of a Klingon ship. A Gorn colony. Some forty-three other species he could identify at a quick glance.

There were seven views of the interior of the *Enterprise,* including a massively worried Scott in command on the bridge.

The holocubes were monitored by automatic equipment. Beyond them were habitats where many species perched, swam, flew, crawled, or disconsolately drew creature warmth from one another in the manner of the caged. A fight was in progress in one cage. A sound-damping screen came down around it, discreetly cutting off the annoyance of mayhem.

Spock turned his focus inward for a long moment and performed the mastery-of-the-unavoidable. He discerned that the full Vulcan had done so earlier and with more thoroughness. Nonetheless, there remained a residue of psychic contamination escaping even from Savaj.

Belen emitted a high, musical call, some part of which would be outside Human hearing range.

Two male Designers appeared from the back of the laboratory, and another crossed on some other errand. They appeared to be the male counterparts of Belen, humanoid, splendidly formed, with classic male definition of muscle, the vestigial featherlike hair black on one and pale gold on the other. They wore, if possible, less than Belen, chiefly a low illusion field that seemed also to serve as belt for tools, weapons, or other accoutrements. But of the usual humanoid or indeed mammalian accoutrements of maleness. Spock could see no definite sign—possibly concealed by the illusion belt or possibly some protective internal storage arrangement.

The two males glanced up, but paid little attention to Belen's subjects. They gave her some casual sign-of-greeting and started to pass on. "You are quite certain as to the time scale?" the slightly smaller fair one said.

"There's no doubt. The rate of increase of hazard is augmented—geometric."

"The Others . . . ?"

"Their studies have arrived at no more definitive conclusion than ours. Their projection of outcome remains the same annihilation of Nome."

Spock's Vulcan brain translated the questioned concept possibilities offered by his translator to the single concept: Nome. The All Whether it was a correct rendition or what the Designers might mean by the Oneness of All, he did not know.

Belen said, "See these. The V-One and -Two subjects, and the link-H's." At least, that was how Spock rendered it.

The two males turned with mild interest. "Which is the V-One?" the dark one said.

Belen indicated. "Its call sound is Savaj, Trath."

Trath moved over to inspect Savaj. They were almost of a size and indeed might very nearly have been cast from the same mold—perhaps not merely physically. They inspected each other with that look of males who command their respective domains, from jungle to starfleet to laboratory.

Trath's look was perhaps that of inspecting a prime bull or a superb fighting animal. No, it was rather more than that, Spock saw.

"This is the one who observed the observers?" Trath queried.

Belen affirmed hands.

"Question it as discussed—under brainstrip, if necessary. Then the others." Trath made a note on a belt recorder.

"Can you afford that?" Savaj said. "A waste of the lives of the only ones who detected your design?"

Trath looked up, surprised. "Once I know, what more could you tell me?" He looked at the little group of subjects more carefully for a moment. "Do not waste my time. You have attracted brief attention over a period of some of your years and decades for certain unusual behavior or representation of certain planetary partial solutions. You, in particular, climbed out of a box and appeared in inappropriate but astutely chosen locations rather too often. It is quite an admirable feat for a subject. But it is a ripple on the pond of forever. I am concerned with the fate of a totality you cannot conceive. You will contribute what you have to give. Do not speak to me of your lives."

He turned, dismissing them with no further word or thought, a scientist bent on a war with a runaway epidemic of a cancer that would end his species. What were rats and rabbits, or even *snarth*, to him?

"Why do the subjects *choose* to return to the danger-aggression zones?" Savaj asked very clearly.

Trath stopped in midstride and turned to look at Savaj.

"Is it possible," Savaj asked, "that the greatness cannot exist without the violence?"

"Who has raised with you such questions?" Trath said dangerously.

"*I* have," Savaj said. "*We* have." He indicated Kirk. "They are implied in the oldest fire myth of these Humans' world." He nodded then toward Spock. "This one, bred to their world and born to mine, went out to the stars to investigate the duality of his heritage, and his soul, in the zone of danger—and greatness. This one"—he indicated McCoy—"is a born healer who chooses to fight death in the battle zone. The three together may be a lesson that neither I nor my world has yet learned fully.

139

If so—neither have *you*. You did not understand their rapport. You found it worth study. And it might even be the lead toward the solution of the Promethean dilemma."

"The Final Question?" the fair Designer translated.

Trath looked very carefully at Savaj, at Kirk, Spock, McCoy. Spock understood that he would now send them either to the brainstrip process or to some test and interrogation intended to solve the riddle the rat had unexpectedly propounded.

"Brainstrippers," Spock remarked, "as a rule, are unsubtle and largely ineffectual against my species." He carefully did not say which species.

Trath turned to look at him, perhaps noting that. "Ours are effectual. I grant, in this case, some possibility of insufficient subtlety." He turned to Belen. "Have them prepared. Bring them when I summon."

He turned and left with the fair one.

"Prepared for *what?*" McCoy asked under his breath.

Kirk took his arm. "I don't think you want to know."

Belen deposited them without ceremony in a keeping cage and left.

Chapter Twenty

Kirk turned on Savaj. "Just what did you pull? Sir."

Fortunately the Vulcan did not pretend to misunderstand him. "I believe you have a saying, Commander. 'First you have to get his attention.' "

Kirk sat down on a perch, a little weakly. It was a while before the Vulcans realized that he was laughing.

They exchanged commiserating looks.

"Yes, *sir!*" Kirk said when he could. "You did *that.* Now what the hell did you *say?*"

Savaj regarded him gravely. "I asked him the question for which the psychologists needed to interrogate the rat. It is, in fact, the most important question raised by the actual early rat studies of your own world, and it has never been truly solved. Nor have we succeeded in asking the rat."

"You mean," McCoy said, "why do the rats run back into Hell's Kitchen?"

Savaj turned to the doctor. "I am unfamiliar with the term, Doctor. But I believe you have understood me."

Kirk looked a question at McCoy. "The old studies," McCoy said tiredly. "Experimenters found increased aggression in rats living under conditions of crowding—the rat equivalent of Human cities, slums, crime areas, tough

141

districts: Hell's Kitchen. Normal, decent, orderly rat behavior broke down. There were rapes, murders, gang fights, a high level of excitement, increased sexual behavior, much more danger and a shocking death rate."

Kirk nodded. "It's been used as an argument for decentralization, even for space-to-person ratios on a starship. But—Hell's Kitchen?"

"The clincher was," McCoy said, "once given a taste of the high life, and high death, when given a choice the rats would run back, to live—or die—in Hell's Kitchen. They did not choose peace, safety, life."

Kirk remembered then; it was a passing scientific oddity that had struck him too, although he had never heard it put in the vivid metaphor of Hell's Kitchen, the toughest slum district of nineteenth- and twentieth-century New York.

"The studies have since been replicated," Spock added, "with many life forms on most worlds. Including, apparently, most otherwise intelligent beings."

Kirk turned to the two Vulcans. "You are saying, sir, that we will all run to the excitement—even to the aggression and the death?"

"Commander," Savaj said, "in your spare time you are a starship Captain."

Kirk winced. "I wouldn't have put it quite that way."

"It was a species of compliment."

Kirk regarded him warily. "Correct me if I'm wrong, sir. Am I hearing a *Vulcan* say that there may be a use —or even a need—for the aggression syndrome? And that it could even be essential to greatness?"

Savaj looked out from the cage for a long moment, then turned back to Kirk. "You are hearing a Vulcan, reluctantly and at the end of more than ten decades of personal and ten centuries of racial belief to the contrary, consider that possibility. In logic I must consider it, even though my own resistance is strong and my life has been spent attempting to keep Vulcan from relearning the attractions and the dangers of what the doctor has called Hell's Kitchen. We Vulcans are much too dangerous a species, if unleashed."

"My God," McCoy said.

Savaj shook his head. "If it is true that the greatness cannot be separated from the aggression, then there is

142

certainly no benevolent design in the universe, Doctor. Nor will it long survive. For if that is truly the case, then every intelligent corporeal species must choose, ultimately, mediocrity—or destruction."

"You think," Kirk said, "that the Designers have arrived at that choice.".

"I think," Savaj said, "that they have foreseen its arrival. And for the first time an intelligent species has conceived the Promethean design of trying to steal the fire of *that* answer from the gods or from the vultures of destruction."

"And if they don't succeed?" Kirk asked softly.

"Then they, and some other all-dimension species which has also reached that point, will pull the universe down on all our heads."

They sat for a long moment in silence, Kirk visualizing the vast and intricate mosaic of an experiment intended to solve that question—a general field theory for intelligent life on a galactic, perhaps a universal scale. And poised somewhere was sufficient power to destroy the totality of the all.

More than once when Earth was still the All for all of Kirk's kind, the species had arrived at the capacity to destroy that All: the early atomic crisis, neutron bombs and doomsday weapons, biological vectors, chemical planet killers. At each critical juncture, two or more superrats dressed in suits or tunics or synth-fields would bare teeth and brandish spears that could now kill a world. And somewhere off in the back-of-beyond was a bushman who had never heard of either superrat and wanted only to make the bush safe for his little democracy—his wife, kids, friends, pets, and starship. If the superrats had come to experiment on the bushman, saying that it might save the world, the bushman would have objected. Yet if the superrats had blown up the world, he would have gone with it—never having heard of the superrats or the problem.

"Admirable analysis, little subject," a voice said behind him.

Kirk turned, not sure whether it was a comment on Savaj's words or his own thoughts.

Belen was there, but it was not she who had spoken. There was another female Designer with her.

And if Belen had struck him as beautiful, this one struck him as dangerous. If fire had been transmuted into woman, this was that woman. There was a sweep of spun-fire, of burnished copper-bronze feather-hair on her head, and she wore body illusion-ornaments or plumage to match. Her eyes were dark shadows opening to bronze-gold flame. But the real fire was inner. He could have warmed his hands at it—or burned them.

He felt his face flush, suspecting that she could read exactly the stirring of an old interest, for which he had not had much time lately. Worse, Belen could probably read it, too—and that struck him as not merely dangerous, but possibly fatal.

The flame-woman laughed low in her throat. "You see? The subject is quite prepared to sell soul, or body, for his friends or his ship. I might even note, he seems recurrently eager to do so."

Belen shrugged hands. "It is a known factor of this one's record, Flaem. It seems unnecessary for you to compel him to demonstrate it yet again."

Flaem—at least the sound was close to that—but Kirk's mind inevitably and persistently translated it as Flame. She turned the burning eyes on him and the eyes laughed. "A good scientist always takes the opportunity to observe at first hand the possibly subtle nuances of behavior. Even Trath has decreed a period of subtlety for these subjects."

"You consider your behavior subtle?" Belen said in her most silver voice.

Flaem laughed. "It is up to the subject to show subtlety." Then she looked at Kirk in cool appraisal. "You have had the temerity to come to us and the gall to condemn us for using lives—and now do you have the nerve to consider making our case for us?"

Kirk felt substantially deflated and more than a little demoralized, but he hoped not to let the flame-one see it. "I'm not very subtle," he said disarmingly. "I'm the bushman with my little bush family and my pet Koala and my primitive starship. But what I have is mine. You may blow it up. But I won't see you play with it. If you want any cooperation from me, you will ask for it—nicely."

The flame-one lifted a brow-feather. "It speaks with some spirit. Interesting."

"It always does," Belen said.

"Have you taught it no manners?"

"It has learned shame. You know that."

Flaem hand-signed affirmation. "Rather more than shame is required." She looked beyond Kirk to McCoy. "Your cagemate is not well. I had better examine him."

"No!" Kirk said quickly. "My other cagemates are attending him. He merely needs a little rest." He looked at Flaem directly. "Perhaps we could continue this conversation elsewhere for a time."

Her eyes laughed. "We could continue." She pointed her wrist-feather at something and the force field at the front of the cage snapped off. "You see," she remarked to Belen, "the subject's response is almost a reflex."

Belen looked at him and past him to McCoy with silver eyes that seemed to hold something of a common decency. "What would you expect?" she said quietly. "He defends his own."

"I expect him to come—" Flaem said.

Kirk resisted an impulse that had little to do with chivalry or sanity and much to do with aggression. But he followed her out. He didn't look back at Spock or Savaj, not wanting to see anything Vulcan faces had to say about it. McCoy started to say, "Jim!" but seemed to be cut off.

Kirk shrugged mentally. There could be worse fates. If he could get past being mad as hell. He let himself be marched between the two women and kept his eye out for the main chance—layout of the place, possible escape route, weapons, whatever. Now that they were here, he devoutly wanted at least some conceivable way out. If nothing else, at least for McCoy. He kept remembering the doctor's gray face, still trying to wisecrack the edge off fear for the rest of them. But McCoy had been through some similar alien hell the first time Kirk had and had had no moment's peace since. Kirk had to give McCoy at least an hour or two and Spock and Savaj some chance to pull him together. Or else the Designers, with an infallible instinct for a weak animal or even with Belen's misplaced attempt at Human decency, might get some idea about putting him out of his misery. And the Designing woman beside him had known that, too well. She had unhesitatingly used it to force him to do what she wanted.

He found Flaem looking at him speculatively, and he now had no interest. They reached what appeared to be

145

some living space area. He could make no sense of the furniture—that thing that he took for a bed was probably a table and possibly an energy fish tank.

Flaem said, "Very well, I see no need to delay the demonstration of capacity further."

Belen stood by and appeared to be rooted more firmly than a silver tree.

"It doesn't," Kirk began, "quite work that way."

Flaem looked at him with some amusement. "Of course it does. Come, little one. You needn't be embarrassed. You have no secrets from me."

Kirk remembered the holograms showing views into the *Enterprise,* including his cabin and including back records of their log. He tried to suppress the thought. Then it occurred to him that it was much worse than that. Those blanked-out periods when the no-mouths had taken him —she could have been, would have been, observing that, reviewing the tapes, or even watching at the time, on the spot, directing the no-mouths' actions, perhaps bringing him here, then sending him back with additional cause for rage that he could not remember.

She stepped closer to him now, reading his consternation, and was amused. He was not amused. He was as close as he ever wanted to come to wanting to kill a woman.

And still her eyes mocked him, taunted him, challenged him. Hell's Kitchen, he thought, without context or logic. And then he smiled at her. "Let's talk this over," he said.

Chapter Twenty-one

Savaj focused within to summon the healing mode for the need of the Human healer. In a Vulcan lifetime there was room for the learning of many disciplines, although not so many as Savaj would have preferred. For one whose life path led to the stars, the discipline of healing wounded and weakened life forms was an early necessity.

Spock, while yet young, already had a certain gift for the healing, Savaj perceived. Spock's touch soothed his old friend McCoy and Savaj perceived that on this rest place Spock made for him they maintained no barbed pretense that it had ever been otherwise.

"Jim!" McCoy said. "Spock—that female four-alarm fire would as soon throw him to the mindstripper as look at him."

"I know, Leonard. I believe he relies, for the moment, on a preference to look at him."

McCoy smiled feebly. "Well, he's gotten us out of more than one kettle of hot water—or jail cell for that matter —by throwing somebody a few curves. I wish I didn't think those two are so advanced that they might just pat him on the head."

"Irrespective of advancement," Savaj remarked objectively, "that did not appear to be the anatomy they would pat." He looked at Spock. "Nor do you appear concerned with the means your friend would use or what he would sell to buy time."

Spock merely looked at him. "That is true, *S'haile*. No more than he would be, given what he buys it for." He put a hand on McCoy's forehead. "Now, Leonard, you must focus on that."

McCoy's blue eyes became grave. "I know, Spock. He thinks I've had it, short of miracles or some pretty spectacular diversion of attention." The eyes closed for a moment. "He may be right, Spock. I'm thinking of all the millions and billions of lives."

"We will yet stop the Designers, Doctor," Spock said. "I do not offer logical evidence for that position. But we are committed to that course."

"Spock, I don't mean *them*. I mean *us*. Billions of little lives. For research alone. When the antivivisectionists tried to stop research on live animals in the nineteenth century, it was maybe a thousand animals in the world. I remember some figure from twenty years before the year two thousand. *One hundred million* laboratory animals per year in the then United States alone—driven insane, suffocated, poisoned, battered, scalded, blinded, radiated, crushed— to death. And eighty-five percent of it was done without any anesthetic. Much of it was for research that was crude, repetitive, the answers already known in school. And it didn't shop there. Food. Furs. And the incalculable cruelty to our *own* kind. Spock, maybe there really *is* a flaw in the mechanism in us, all of us—a fatal flaw. The inhumanity . . . I've done it too, Spock. With my own hands."

McCoy held up his surgeon's hands and they were shaking. Spock covered them with one of his own. "There is nothing in those hands, Doctor, but the antidote for whatever flaw we fight here. I am not certain what answer we will find, but I know it requires your survival." Spock paused a moment, then added quietly, "As do I."

McCoy looked up in surprise. "That's some bedside manner you have, Captain Spock."

Savaj also looked sharply at Spock. "Indeed, your recent behavior is virtually a catalog of Human influence on a Vulcan—down to a certain release of aggression and other emotions. Perhaps you had better let me attend the Doctor." Spock made no comment, but permitted himself to be displaced. "In all logic, Doctor," Savaj said, "your predecessors were dealing at that period with a rate of cancer that had gone in decades from negligible to one out of four. It was to go to one out of two—in places nearly to one out of one—before environmental and medical research—sometimes on animals—reversed the trend. The increase of other diseases was also epidemic. Certain environmental trends, if not detected through animal and other research, would swiftly have rendered the planet uninhabitable for your life form and all others— and all of the little lives would have died with you in their hundreds of trillions. The same is true of most worlds at some point. That is the Designers' position now. And if they go, we go. We must, in logic, offer them some other argument than the pain of mice—when their children are dying."

"Admiral Savaj," McCoy said, "the strictest prohibition of Vulcan is against causing suffering and death, even to the least animal form, even to complex plants."

Savaj nodded. "It is a recent luxury, Doctor, won at great expense. The first right of a species is survival. And that is *your* priority now." Savaj put his hands on McCoy's face. "If you permit," he murmured, and without disturbing the upper levels of consciousness slipped in to the lower brain consciousness to activate the brain's own chemical painkillers. The Humans had discovered such chemicals at the root of placebo effects and called them endorphins. Vulcans had also identified the similar internal endochemicals against shock, stress—against certain aspects of the body's specific death chemical itself. Hence the two-hundred-fifty-year life span, perhaps still to be extended.

There was a severe limit to what one consciousness could do for another in that way. Chiefly it was a self-healing process, learned at some cost. But what Vulcan could do for Human, Savaj did now for this healer whose courage drove him beyond his capacity.

The Human was a frail vessel. Neither he nor the other one, Kirk, seemed large enough to Savaj, nor sturdy enough, to carry the weight of what he had seen them do or endure. It was an illogical form of stubbornness they possessed. Their species had many failings, such as willful disobedience. It was unduly trusting in its willingness to

Chapter Twenty-two

Kirk watched Flaem switch off the holo screen which showed Spock, Savaj and McCoy. She stretched languorously. "Your cagemates also have interesting attributes."

"Yes." He let himself say it somewhat absently, as if concentrating on discovering again that feathers could tickle. They could. But chiefly he was still worried sick. McCoy was not out of the woods as far as the Designers were concerned. Kirk expected Trath to send for Spock, Savaj, or himself at any moment for the mindstripper or otherwise.

And he wasn't certain that he had made any points here—certainly nothing that would protect him and his little bush family. He felt a little foolish.

She was amused, she was pleased with him. And she was about a thousand years old. Maybe ten times that. Maybe no age he could conceive. The flame-feathered body, the magnificent sculptured face were ageless. They might have been thirty in his terms. But they had seen everything, known everything, a thousand thousand times. She had been right. He had no secrets from her. He never had had.

"Say it aloud, little one. Your thoughts are rather fragile."

He caught himself feeling too warm again. And he

knew that it was useless, worse than dangerous, to lie to her. "I'm embarrassed."

"Why?"

"You have known perhaps a thousand dimensions, sailed them as I sail stars. How many ports have you known and how many life forms, great and small? I have, on occasion, known someone to whom it was all new, but to you it must be all old."

She stood up and drew him after her to what was perhaps a window. Or perhaps it was merely a hologram. Perhaps something else entirely. It seemed to open on a sky that was not lavender, but the color of her feather-hair. The clouds were gold. The spires of what might have been a world-city were rising into the fire-sky as spirals of rainbow and crystal. Bright wings lifted tiny figures into the sky. They were not the feathered wings with which her remotest bird-mammal ancestors might have been born, but wings born of mind, which could carry their Designers to heights yet unreached, and beyond that to dimensions still unknown, and to the problem standing unsolved at the world's end.

"Home," he said, not as a question.

She nodded. "By now the All is our home. But this begins."

"And it is threatened. By whom?"

"You would not know, nor does it matter. The Others who threaten are . . . sufficient unto the ending of the beginning and of all things. If they are no worse than we, they are no better. They, too, share that fault, which the outbox V-One specimen has defined as Promethean." She turned to him rather coldly. "He is quite right, you know, specimen or not. The first right of a species is survival."

"It troubles you to do this to the small lives," Kirk divined.

The flame-eyes hardened. "No. It does not trouble me. Throughout the universe are the lives I defend, of my own kind and kinds that will become great. Perhaps even including your own. And under our feet, as under yours, are the tiny lives we are not equipped to notice and the small lives on which we would smile, if we could. Sometimes we do, even as we speed up a natural process here, apply a catalyst there, weed a garden somewhere else. And if some are hurt and some die, we still defend even their lives against the ending that would be forever."

She touched his temple. "You have thought of the bushman. Would you wish us to leave your bush family alone until that day when it vanishes in the flame of forces you have never conceived?"

He considered it for a long moment. "I do not accept that that is the only alternative. As what I am, I would wish for the chance to know the problem, study, learn, grow—until perhaps together we could take your finger off the doomsday button."

She looked at him in amusement. "You do not lack for temerity, little one. It is *that* which is your youth."

He nodded. "Callow. Obstreperous. Unmannered. Unconvinced. Youth has its price—and its uses."

"Yes," she said. "It can make everything that was old new again."

She leaned forward and brushed his lips with hers.

"I would not have believed you could do that," she said, "and it changes nothing."

She turned her back on him to look at the homeworld. "You may report outside to Belen, who will take you to Trath."

"Flaem," he said. But she did not turn to him.

"Could you see me put under the mindstripper? *Now?*"

Then she did turn, but there was nothing in her for him. "That which I do, I can do. If I make a pet of a laboratory animal, I pay the price, but I do not exempt it, or myself, from reality."

"You mean," he said, *"it pays the price."* He started to turn on his heel, but she caught his arm and turned him to face the screen. The bright-winged fliers in the sky of the homeworld shriveled in flames, one by one, and the rainbow city began to burn. Then the whole homeworld dissolved in fire.

He looked at Flaem in horror. "It's not happening," he said tightly. "Thought projection? Illustration? Vision? Not—history?"

She looked now like some figure set with flaming sword at the east of Eden. "Future history," she said. "The precognon varies only in detail, unless the nature of being is changed at its root. Do you ask me to set your one life against *that?*"

153

He looked at the roiling emptiness that would be the end of her beginning. "If it were only my life and that would stop it—I have sometimes offered it, not happily, for less. But it is not only my life, and you have not asked, but taken."

The fire-eyes flared with anger. "Leave my presence." He turned and left.

Kirk found Belen waiting for him in the outer chamber. He realized suddenly that she could, of course, read his shock and his anger—and knew the cause of it. Worse, perhaps she could read everything he had done or said. And for how long?

"Do your people not have the concept of privacy?" he said, then realized that he was taking his shock and his anger out on her, when she had showed him chiefly decency.

"They have the concept of benign neglect of the warning space of equals. Do small life consider that they have warning space?"

He sighed. "We try. Among my people that which is between male and female would most often be within a private warning space."

She looked surprised. "That would eliminate many options and much esthetic appreciation."

He looked at her feathery coolness and finally smiled at her. "You know, you're right. I'm sorry I snapped at you. Something I could not stop has shaken me. Could we walk, talk?"

"I have a time frame," she said.

"To take me to Trath?"

She made hands of affirmation.

"Until then?" he said very quietly.

She turned and led him into a vast indoor garden, its private nooks sheltered by the exotic plants of a galaxy. "Belen," he said. "I begin to see that your species feels its own desperation. But is there no one among the Designers who is troubled by the use of the small lives? Is there no one who argues some other option?"

She stood with him under a slow fall of floating flowers. Tiny, exotic bits of living petal-jeweled life drifted down onto their hair, their feathers. "There is perhaps almost no one who is *not* troubled at some level. Even the meat eaters of your own world shun the slaughterhouse. Many would not with their own hands do what must be done if they are to have flesh, fur, feathers, knowledge. Some would not do it even for knowledge that would mean life to their species. We . . . have chosen to do so."

There was some faint stress of hesitation on the "we," which Kirk caught. "Have *you* yourself chosen?"

She lifted her head. "I have not chosen otherwise. Not irrevocably."

"Then there *is* an option."

Something seemed to fall away from her and he saw suddenly the steel behind the silver. "I have argued one. Some have accepted, but it is a reluctant option and of little use unless all agree."

"Who stands against you?"

"At their head? You have known her."

"Flaem. Is that part of some reason that made her come for me?"

"You are not slow, are you?" She reached out and brushed a drift of flowers off his forearm. "She wished perhaps to remind me with some vividness that we *are* corporeal life—flesh and blood."

Kirk smiled. "I never doubted it." Then he saw the look in her eyes. "Is there some question?"

"That is *the* question, small one. For us. Ultimately perhaps even for you. Do you know of any life form you have encountered that seemed to you to have solved the Promethean problem?"

Kirk thought about it carefully. Vulcans—if you did not count fights to the death in the arena of marriage or challenge and that always present level of underlying dangerousness that must be mastered lest it master them. And was anybody counting the level of pain that had sent Spock off to Vulcan for three years to try to cut off half his life? No. Not Vulcans. It was a magnificent and terrible effort at a solution, and still it was partial. Humans? Still less. Although it was his gut feeling, doubtless illogical and indefensible, that the sheer cussedness of his own species, despite its record of atrocity, would ultimately allow it to muddle through. The Human species would, in defiance of all logic, climb out of water onto land, climb from sky to stars to dimension-sailing, and on some million-year day even solve—with the strange alien brothers it would have picked up on the way—the Promethean problem.

But he did not know how. Nor did he know any species that had. Then he amended that. "I know of no solution I would want to copy." He caught her wrist from his arm suddenly and held it hard. "The Organians," he said. "You are not thinking of the Organian solution? Energy beings, no bodies, no passion—"

He broke off.

"Is it so terrible, then?" she said, but he saw in her eyes that she knew the full meaning of that choice. "Those whom you call Organians, and some like them, have had thousands of years of unchanging peace, a species of life —at the expense of no living being and at the mercy of none." She looked at him levelly. "Unless we solve the Promethean problem within a time span that we measure in moments, that ceases to be merely an ethical option and becomes our only chance of survival. More, it will be the only chance of survival of all your little lives and of the universe. Although even our choice may not save you from the Others."

He looked down at her hand in his, the fine feathered wrist, the delicate strength, the decency almost written in the hand that would stay itself from taking life even at the cost of dissolution.

He knew that he should encourage her, throw whatever weight he had behind her lone fight for a moral solution. He should do it for the survival of his own kind. If the Designers went the Organian route, they presumably would practice a similar benign neglect. And it might be a million years before some other conflict between species that retained the body became powerful enough to destroy the All.

And nonetheless his whole body and soul rebelled at that solution, and he saw that hers did too.

He lifted the wrist to his lips and kissed it. She would perhaps distrust what he had brought to Flaem, or for what reason. But there had to be some acknowledgment of her fight and of how much she would lose if she won.

Finally he no longer cared what she might distrust. He tipped her face back until flowers fell on it from his hair and kissed her.

For a moment she stiffened with the resolution of her

commitment. But she was a house divided against itself, and she knew it as well as he. Her lips softened and some light, feathery touch of her mind reached for his. *It is still the only way*. The words were not words but a sadness, a bird mourning flight, mourning the death of flight in fire.

It is not a way for us. He tried to put into it not only male and female, but the climbing onto land and to stars, the unlimited striving. It was a passion he knew she must share if her species would tackle the Promethean question.

It was some time before he sensed a presence behind him.

Kirk remained transfixed for a moment. He could only assume that Belen would have known of someone's approach. The Designers seemed to know almost everything —even the future. Was there some way in which Belen had wanted this to be seen?

He detached himself with as much aplomb as he could muster under the circumstances and turned to face the new presence.

It was Flaem. And Trath. Kirk could not offhand think which one he would less like to have seen there. He suspected that the combination was fatal, perhaps literally and immediately.

Something in Flaem's coppery eyes suggested a touch of green. That, however, could not be right. Jealous of a subject? Even a pet?

Kirk inclined his head gravely, a token of acknowledgment. "Flaem. *S'haile* Trath."

Trath's lowering frown developed a touch of interest. "The accompanying title designation does not translate. I sense its intent is . . . respect."

"An ancient Vulcan title of respect, *S'haile*, which is all I know of it except the stature of the man who bears it. It strikes me you bear a similar stature and weight of command here."

"You mean the V-One subject. Interesting. Do you arrogate to yourself the right to call me by a title of respect that compares me to a laboratory animal? Or are you merely trying to distract me from the fact that an animal has touched a female of my species?"

"I was rather hoping to distract you," Kirk said.

For a moment there was some flicker in Trath's black eyes. Amusement? No. He was, pointedly, *not amused*.

"Is it forbidden?" Kirk tried innocently.

"It is not contemplated." Trath turned to Belen. "You will explain to me the research that requires the advocate of dissolution of body to embrace a small life?"

Belen stood her ground. "It was not research."

"Then it was madness," Trath said. "A scientist may fondle a rabbit. One does not take it to one's bower."

Belen looked at Flaem. "Nor to one's bed. No. That is quite true."

"The habitual reflexes of a long-studied specimen are a proper subject of study," Flaem said flatly.

"That was what you started," Belen said. "Not what you finished. You were not responding to him as a small life. You were responding to him as a man—as male of kindred stature, even across a million-year gulf."

"Perhaps that is what *you* were doing, Belen," Flaem said, but Kirk saw something in the flame-eyes that had been hit by the argument.

"Yes," Belen said firmly, "it was."

Flaem laughed. "All will see how prepared you are to give up the body."

"Which was, perhaps, your aim, Flaem. I have never claimed to be prepared—merely compelled. That has not changed. We consume lives. Even these small ones with their own frailties find us guilty. But they do not now use lives of moral stature and ethical sensibility. This small life made his case against my position with his body knowing fully that it was against his own interest."

The others were silent for a moment, turning to Kirk as if inspecting him with some care.

Flaem made sign of negation. "He made a similar argument to me quite in his own interest. Do not confuse the reflex of a rabbit with moral stature."

"That is more than sufficient," Trath said. "Reflexes are not in question. Neither his nor yours." He looked at Belen and Flaem without pleasure. "The subject will be examined properly."

He turned to Kirk. "Come."

Chapter Twenty-three

Kirk followed Trath.

The controlling Designer reminded him in some peculiar way of someone he knew well. He had thought that it was Savaj, and perhaps it still was, or perhaps both shared some essential quality of someone else. Sarek? Nogura? Something of all of those, perhaps, but also others out of a lifetime against the unknown. Not all who shared that quality had been friends. One, perhaps the greatest one, he had marooned forever on an unreachable planet. Now —he could have wished for Omne's mind against this riddle.*

"There are minds in this galaxy," Kirk said as they moved, "that are superior to mine. Older. Wiser. Tougher. More controlled. There are some that have mastered what I could not attempt. There are some that could master *me* —and perhaps even challenge *you* on some level. I have known one or two. I have known at least one who would attempt a problem of Promethean scope. I could not reach him now, but you could. Have you consulted no one in this galaxy?"

Trath looked at him as if he read beyond the words. "Do

*The Price of the Phoenix and The Fate of the Phoenix, by S. Marshak and M. Culbreath not be deceived by appearance, subject. We retain the body, the size, the form by choice, after some aeons of experimentation, for some of the reasons, among others, that you argued with Belen—and elsewhere—in your elementary way. But we are as far beyond your most advanced contemporary as he is beyond an unborn kitten."

"I would not be quite certain of that, S'haile," Kirk said. "I have known enemies whom I considered to be of moral stature. I am not certain it is a mark of stature or advancement to discount the possibility of learning from the enemy—or even from the kitten. I have on occasion learned something from one or the other—even the newborn kitten. New life has not yet learned what is impossible."

Trath stopped before a door and looked at him. "That is its fault, not its virtue."

"Then why pick it up out of the box?"

The black eyes scored him a point. "When one exhausts the possible, one begins on the impossible."

"What remains impossible to your advancement?" Kirk said. "Even Vulcans who are still young to your kind have given up the using of feeling lives—and they control aggression. Why not you?"

"Vulcans," Trath said, "stay out of Hell's Kitchen. Do you not suppose that we tried that long ago? It was a Vulcan who posed to you the question of greatness—and a half-Vulcan who has followed you all over Hell's Kitchen." He signaled the door and gestured Kirk through it.

Kirk saw a sophisticated private laboratory in which Trath looked shockingly at home. Holodisplays monitored uncounted experiments. And there was sophisticated equipment, including, doubtless, the mindstripper. Civil argument left Kirk and he knew what Trath called forth in him: the desire to kill.

Spock regarded the woman with some care. It would perhaps have been more prudent to attempt to thought-summon the silver bird.

Belen was, at least, a vibration of some sympathy.

In some curious manner Spock felt more personal affinity with the living flame. Perhaps he felt kinship as a scientist himself, or perhaps as a latter-day and somewhat reluctant warrior who nevertheless had chosen to defend what he did defend. Or possibly he saw in her also one who had developed a taste for the fire of Hell's Kitchen. It was Spock's flaw, which had divided him to his soul; and in the end even the three-year attempt to give it up had proved futile.

"Flaem," Spock said, "the scientist who intends to sacrifice a laboratory animal does not take it home and hand-feed it, talk to it, see to it if it is disconsolate. At the least you have done that. It would be my conjecture that, as others before you, you have also seen a particular being's worth, across whatever gulf, and stretched out your hand to it. To him. He will die now unless your hand is raised to shelter him."

She regarded him with the flame eyes and did not speak.

"Then . . . let me go to him," Spock said.

"Do you imagine that you are able here to shelter him yourself?"

"No," Spock said. "But I am able to join him."

"In death?"

"You hold the alternative. I have none."

"You consider him your responsibility?"

"I am responsible. I consider him my friend." He used the Vulcan word, which meant more. *T'hyla.* Brother. Her translator or her thought would render all the connotations. Savaj would hear the Vulcan.

She merely looked at him with the eyes that were the color of the Humans' hellfire. Then she opened the cage.

Kirk fought his way up through sheeted layers of fire—the rage, the shame, the helplessness again, the wish to annihilate all Trath's kind. He cursed himself for a fool. Had he supposed because he could speak some kind of language to a Designer that he would not be used for their purpose?

Even the poor damn chimpanzees who first learned to talk sign language had spoken of their feelings, their pain, of mourning for a dead infant. They had been heard. Nobody had canceled the experiment.

He fought to come up out of the flames. Did he have any mind left? Did anyone care?

How had his species survived the loathing that must

have been broadcast at them by their billions of helpless victims, their own kind and all others?

He jerked himself up out of it by some savage effort of will. A hatred of that magnitude would corrode the soul. It would curdle the psychic atmosphere. And if it reached the Vulcans when they were powerless to reach him . . . Kirk cut it off and opened his eyes. Trath was releasing him from the light restraint field and the electrodes at his temples. He sagged and would have fallen, but the Designer lowered him to some pallet. Kirk shook off the touch and fought to be able to rise.

He had made it to his knees when Spock and Savaj came in. He fought not to betray their entrance with his eyes. Trath's back was to them and the Vulcans moved with the silence and stealth of the desert *snarth*.

"You observe," Trath remarked to Kirk, "how easily the aggression threshold can be lowered. You wish to kill me, do you not?"

"Devoutly," Kirk said, holding his eyes and trying to hold his full attention. "Would you expect otherwise?"

"I expect exactly what I get," Trath said. "I so arrange it. V-subjects, you are on time."

Spock jumped for him, but Trath smashed the Vulcan back casually. Then he turned with the light stasis field in hand. Spock and Savaj were stopped, held.

Flaem came in with McCoy and Kirk saw that Spock looked at her in a way that should have dropped her where she stood.

"As ordered," she said to Trath. Belen entered behind her without comment.

McCoy came to Kirk and was not stopped, as if they considered him not necessary to notice. "Jim!" he murmured.

Kirk motioned him to silence. "Don't give them anything, Bones." He got to his feet.

Trath turned to him. "There is only one thing we require."

"What?" Kirk said.

"You."

Kirk looked at him bitterly. "You have me."

"That is true. I wish to keep you for a purpose that is not served by mere possession. You have proved to be an exceptional specimen. Your command record in the

162

terms of your own kind is singular. You are also the focus of that rapport which did not break with the test-to-destruction. You are the first subject to achieve being picked up by choice. Your mind recording is interesting, and you have had an unexpected, if modest, effect on certain persons here. You will do as a sample of this galaxy—a small but select sample."

"Do you mean," Kirk said, "that you will let the others go? My friends? My ship?"

"Subject," Trath said, "I mean your galaxy."

Kirk straightened slowly. "Forever?" he said. "Free and clear? No experiments, no experimenters? No gardens weeded? Just go?"

"We have elsewhere. Your particular bush family can be safe for as long as the All endures—until we die or prevail."

"Or perhaps," Flaem said, "if your friends return to give warning, it will be your kind that will solve the Last Question."

Kirk turned to Trath. "How can I know they would be safe?"

"You are in no position to bargain or inquire. I offer the flat option. Once."

Kirk knew the tone of finality. And he had no option. He opened his mouth to answer.

"Mr. Kirk, you will not speak," Spock ordered flatly.

Kirk looked at him, torn. In truth there was, for once, nothing he wanted more than to obey. Except—

"Spock," he said, "I can't *not*."

"You *will not speak*." Spock turned very slowly in the stasis field to face Trath. "You command; you must recognize command responsibility. His life is not his to give. It is mine. His policy has always been lives for defense, but not one life for tribute. Nor do I buy freedom with his life."

"Not even the freedom of the galaxy, Captain Spock?" Trath said.

"Not of the universe," Spock said. "It has been tried—the appeasement of evil. The line is drawn at one life or it is not drawn."

Kirk heard his own argument coming back at him. "Spock," he said, "it is a small price even for lives in this

163

room, let alone a galaxy. No one can offer another's life as hostage. But he can offer his own."

"Not when it is under my command," Spock said flatly. "Trath, *I* will go with you."

"*You* will not serve."

"It was *I*," Savaj cut in, "who ordered the *Enterprise* into your hands to draw you out with that unique rapport, which I knew you would have to study. The responsibility is mine."

Kirk locked eyes with the full Vulcan for a long moment. So it had always been his plan. He had coolly used a rapport that by his standards as *V'Kreeth* should never have existed. And now they would all pay for his decision.

"If a life is forfeit, it is mine," Savaj said. "I offer it."

"Unacceptable," Trath said.

"It was I who saw your purpose."

Trath shrugged. "Interesting, but unavailing. Your choice for Vulcan, if not for yourself, has been to avoid the very temptation of evil. You have made a separate peace. It is proper. It is moral. And your species is saved from sterility only by a splendid and terrible stubbornness that at times fortunately overcomes your logic. Unfortunately, it also ultimately breaks down your suppression of aggression, explosively, when you are confronted with confrontation over the essential. No, *V'Kreeth*, not you."

"Then," Savaj said, "I will have to require Captain Spock to permit Mr. Kirk's offer of himself as hostage for this galaxy."

Chapter Twenty-four

Kirk saw Spock turn in the stasis field to Savaj with an effort that looked as if it would snap something.

"I am the commander in the field," Spock said. "That is unacceptable to me."

"There is no other logical alternative," Savaj said. "We are powerless to fight, resist, escape—or report. We leave the Federation we have sworn to defend, and the galaxy, defenseless and unwarned, to their destruction. If the experiment proceeds, this galaxy will die long before the destruction of the All. Much of it within days, weeks, months. Billions and trillions of lives of our own kind and all others will die. We have not that right. Mr. Kirk has not the right to defy you, nor we to order his sacrifice. But you must permit his offer."

"S'haile," Spock said. "I am in command mode. In my estimation your logic is correct, but your premise is wrong. I declare unalterable opposition."

It had the sound of a Vulcan formula and appeared to have that effect on Savaj. "Ka-vi-fe," he said in a tone Kirk had not heard since the arena on Vulcan.

"Ka-vi-fe," Spock answered in the same tone.

Trath turned up a control on the stasis projector. The two Vulcans froze in a pose of challenge.

It was then that Kirk understood that the stasis field itself must also include some effect that stripped down the veneer of civilization, lowered some threshold of aggression.

The two Vulcans were unalterably opposed on the issue. But would they, on their own, have arrived at a point of physical confrontation? No. Something Trath had done had released in them that reversion to the ancient code, which could still be used on Vulcan to deal with the instincts that came down from the time of the Beginning.

"Release them," Kirk said. "I have made my position clear. Beam them to the *Enterprise* and let me see them clear. I will stay with you."

Trath shook his head. "It is not that simple, subject. I wish you to see that even the Vulcan solution breaks down when the stakes are essentials."

"Under your mind control," Kirk snapped. "It proves nothing."

Trath gestured with the stasis transmitter. "Merely a modest inhibition releaser and impulse accelerator. It does not create the effect, merely brings it to the surface."

"If we are able to keep it off the surface," Kirk said, "that's all we need. A sober alcoholic is still an alcoholic. He just doesn't drink—or kill—today. You can't say the cure failed if you trigger him by forcing a drink down his throat."

"Subject Kirk," Trath said, "the universe is designed to force the drink of aggression down our most sober throats. The stimulation, the excitement, the vividness, the danger, the heightened sensuality, the risk—haven't you known it all along? Hell's Kitchen is an addiction."

Trath pushed a button on the transmitter and he, the Vulcans, the two Designer women, and McCoy vanished from the laboratory.

Kirk looked around, shaken. Was this the beginning of his solitary captivity? The acceptance of his offer? Had Trath beamed the other captives to the *Enterprise* and himself and the women to other tasks, leaving Kirk to take up again at his leisure? Or had he merely disposed of the Vulcans and McCoy? It would be easy enough to show Kirk an illusion or nothing at all.

Kirk felt desolation setting in. It was one thing to make

the decision you had to make and another to live with it for a lifetime.

He cut himself off and got moving. There was still supposed to be a way out of any box.

He inspected the various hologram displays, looking for anything useful. The *Enterprise* views remained unchanged. The holograms had no controls he could see. But at the end of an aisle was a windowlike display that looked like the precognition display in Flaem's quarters.

He went to it. It had no obvious controls either. He tried to focus his thoughts, search for Spock, Savaj, McCoy. Focus ahead. Would they survive? Was there a way to get them out? How?

Suddenly he was seeing the mirror-canyon with its thousand-foot cliffs and its fall of diamonds, its tracery of silver trees. It looked like the lower end of the canyon, near the entrance where they had come in from the ordinary hell of Helvan.

He saw himself. He was supporting Spock, all but carrying him, and it looked as if he had been doing it for a long time. Savaj was behind them, but Kirk couldn't tell why he wasn't helping Spock. McCoy moved with a glazed look, but moved. Kirk could sense his own exhausted elation. A few more feet—

Then the picture on the screen clouded, wavered, snapped. Nothing he could do would bring it back. But it had showed a *chance*. Despite all their sophistication, the Designers must have some blind spot.

The laboratory began to shimmer in front of him and he recognized the dissolution feeling of the Designer transporter. Where was Trath taking him?

Chapter Twenty-five

Kirk found himself beside Trath in a group of Designers who were looking down into a tank-arena that held —what?

The two Vulcans stood in the tank, immobile, stripped down to *asumi* loincloths—but both of them half again their normal size.

"What have you done to them?" Kirk asked.

Trath turned to him blandly. "You would think of it as a kind of enlarging pantograph. The primitive version can enlarge or reduce a drawing. Ours can enlarge a body, while making significant modifications in it, such as a species of armoring. It is not true armoring. It is merely protection of the vital. The body still feels the blow, it can be damaged, but all bones and tissues are strengthened so that damage is usually repairable."

Kirk realized that he was looking at Trath in horror.

"It is a game, subject Kirk—the ultimate game for which all of your species' aggression and territorial games are a poor substitute. They are believed to provide some releases for pent-up aggression, although they may also stimulate the taste for it. This is Battle to the Death— usually without actual death or prolonged disability."

"Get them out of there," Kirk said.

"No."

"I will not be the cause of this. Get them out or I withdraw my offer."

"Your offer was gallant," Trath said, "but necessary only for their ears. I require no consent. Possession suffices."

"Then you would not have kept your bargain?"

"Oddly enough, I would have, and will, but for my own reason."

"Then my offer stands, if you let them go now."

Trath made sign of negation. "I wish to see this. I wish you to see it."

"Why?" Kirk said bitterly. "You can see everything, know everything in advance anyway. I do not know now why you even need experimentation. You must know how it will all come out."

"No," Trath said. "That is not the nature of precognition. It can predict with high accuracy what is within the concept of the possible of the one who foresees. But every living being has a stake in its own pattern of belief, thought, reflex, expectation. If its pattern of belief is not right, it cannot live."

"You are saying we all have blind spots—even you?"

Trath looked at him with a peculiar expression, as if discovering something new. He made a sign of affirmation. "We have contrived the blind-upon-blind experimental design, subject, precisely in the effort to defeat our own blind spots. As a rule, a man—or a species—would rather die than be proved wrong. We seek to defeat that process."

Kirk tried to put down the rage he could not shake, to focus on a certain grudging respect for the intellect he sensed here. "With that I can agree, in principle at least. Let them go and I will join you in that effort. Not the using of lives, but the attempt to break out of the box."

"You must see the whole of the box." Trath flicked a switch and the two Vulcans were freed of the stasis immobility. They seemed to pick up from the moment of challenge where they had left off. They made the *asumi* sign of encounter to death.

"Spock!" Kirk called. "Savaj! It is a test. Don't give them this!"

But he saw that they were beyond hearing or speech.

170

The two Vulcans went for each other like two berserkers from the beginning of time—or its end.

McCoy shook off Belen's supporting hand and made a fast move through the Designers to the edge of the tank beside Jim. He caught Kirk's arm and narrowly restrained the move he had divined. Kirk had started to jump down into the tank between the two Vulcan behemoths. He would have shaken off anyone else, McCoy knew, but he stopped for McCoy.

"If it'd do any good, I'd jump myself," McCoy said. "They wouldn't even know you."

"Spock might."

"They'd break you in half."

Then they could not talk. The Vulcans had closed with each other and it was not the *asumi* practice with pulled punches and illustration of skill. It was what Kirk had called *K'asumi*—the deadliest fighting discipline in the known galaxy. Its highest form could only be summoned against a trained equal. By any name it was lethal. And given Vulcan strength, even against Vulcan durability, any single blow could have been fatal. Under natural conditions one *would* have been, probably within seconds. A hand edge to the throat, a sword hand to the solar plexus, a heel of hand that would have driven the nasal bone into the brain. As a doctor, McCoy knew the actual consequences of even Human unarmed combat skills—better than he wanted to.

He never wanted to see Vulcans fight. But this was some terrible apotheosis of all combat. There was nothing of starships here. This was the original, primordial clash of prime males over territory, dominance, whatever. Maybe the need was in the clash itself. This was Hell's Kitchen on wheels. And it had not even the mercy of the body's eventual inability to endure.

"Stop it!" McCoy snarled at Trath. "They'll kill each other. Don't you know those two won't quit?"

"Yes."

McCoy saw Savaj's size and heft telling against Spock's more slender strength. A hundred years of training the older, full Vulcan Savaj would have. He was driving Spock back against this edge of the tank. Spock's back was against the wall.

Then Spock made his stand. McCoy did not know what

171

he used for muscle, but he used it. It was the stand of a man who could not possibly win, but could not, at any cost, lose.

It was killing both of the Vulcans. They were ten feet tall. They shook the tank. They came together with bone-jarring force. Even the armoring of the pantograph effect was not enough protection now.

Suddenly Kirk slipped out of McCoy's grasp and went over the edge into the tank. It was too swift even for Trath to stop him. McCoy yelled, "Jim!" But he saw Kirk quite deliberately throw himself between the two behemoth Vulcans.

The two were aware only of some unexpected presence, and Savaj started to brush it aside—with a swipe that was the cuff of a Kodiak bear. It caught Kirk a glancing blow in the ribs and McCoy thought it cracked bone. He rolled in the diamond sand, then somehow got up and got between them.

McCoy saw it then. Kirk's only chance between the two armored crushers was to communicate his living presence, his vulnerability. If instinct could work against life, it could work for it. If there was real kinship of kind here, across whatever gulf, even great fighting bulls might stop for a moment to protect the small one. And if they did, even for a moment. then perhaps the great Vulcan brains could override the blood-haze of instinct to remember a starship and a thousand years' peace.

McCoy saw the Vulcans stop, transfixed. The alien mind effect was profound. They were deep into the kill mode. And with whatever mind they had left, the issue between them was one neither could yield.

McCoy saw Savaj's eyes finally focus on Kirk. They were the eyes of the Starfleet Admiral committed to defend a galaxy. And somewhere behind the eyes was a hundred-years pattern of the warning to stay out of the kitchen. a thousand years of peace bought at that price. Somewhere was the *V'Kreeth* with his private hundred-years war for that peace, against this very threat to it. And drawn to the surface now was the Promethean fault in the man who had detected it.

But this was a Vulcan. And this *was* the mind that had detected the Prometheus Design.

McCoy saw an effort at mastery that he thought snapped

every psychic mooring the full Vulcan had ever had. Those things that they had seen Spock learn over a decade and try to unlearn at Gol came to Savaj now. His hand was on Spock's shoulder, forgotten, and it closed until even the armored bones threatened to snap. But the Vulcan's other hand, now on Kirk's shoulder, did not close to break Human bones.

McCoy saw Spock also fight for mastery, but this time it was not the fight for Kolinahr, but the fight to span two worlds. Whatever Spock had learned in ten years came to him now, not only from Vulcan. Spock stood quiet, barely on his feet, but unyielding.

Savaj's eyes finally looked at Kirk with full sanity. Then he looked up out of the tank at Trath.

"No. What is done to the least is done to all. What is done to the best is not to be allowed. We do not yield him."

Trath looked down at him. "Nor do I."

He tapped a control and Savaj crumpled slowly to his knees in the diamond sand of the tank. Spock dropped as if poleaxed.

Then McCoy felt the dissolution effect and found himself back in a cage—a separate cage.

Eventually Kirk was thrown into a cage like a used animal. There was some figure lying crumpled in a dark corner of it.

He crawled over to it, trying not to pull ribs loose, not even sure if it was one of his party. If it was Spock, alive and in any kind of shape, Kirk had music to face for his last couple of stunts too. He had made his offer when ordered not to. And he didn't even know what you called jumping into that tank. Worse, he didn't know what Spock would call it. He was piling up quite a record for mutiny. He wouldn't have taken it and he didn't expect Spock to. But he wasn't up to any music just now. He had faced Trath. It was enough.

But the cold chill in him was that he would find Spock or Savaj dead. He touched a shoulder in the dark and felt the power and heft of Savaj. Alive. Returned to his normal size. Kirk shook him. He was not unconscious, but he seemed to Kirk in some state of shock. It was, perhaps, the aftereffect of Trath's reply to Savaj's defiance.

Or was some part of it the psychic shock of that very effort—in defiance not merely of Trath but of his own pattern?

He was aware of Kirk but he did not respond. Kirk started to put a hand on a shoulder, drew it back. The full Vulcan would not want it. Kirk had imposed his needs enough.

"You are hurt," Savaj said.

"I'm alive." He tried for a tone he did not feel, but the strain crept through. He tried again. "I am well enough, sir. Better than could be expected."

Savaj's voice was tired. "Mr. Kirk, you have a gift for understatement." He made a place for Kirk beside him, propped himself up against the wall.

Kirk heard a sound in the cage. Before he could place it or move, something was bending over him in the darkness. He started up. A hand closed over his mouth—and it was strong but soft. Some hint of dim light caught a gleam of silver as he caught also a faint perfume of skin he knew.

It was Belen.

The Vulcan had started to move and Kirk stopped him with a hand. Belen signaled Kirk's mouth to silence, released it, and for one moment found it with her lips. Then she was up and pulling him to his feet. He signaled the Vulcan to follow and allowed her to lead them out of dark into dark.

He thought of the look on Spock's face in Trath's laboratory when he learned that Flaem had seemed to help them only to deliver the two Vulcans to Trath. This could be another trick, trap, test. He was so infernally tired of tests!

But he would take the chance for the same reason that Spock would: it was the only game in town. For himself there was the lingering hope that the hope was real, that the decency that he had sensed and tried to stir in Belen had really come to their aid. Even if it was only the gesture of a child running away to hide a pet lamb from its fate . . .

She opened the force field of another cell. Kirk felt his way into it, finally found and silenced McCoy. Then he found what was under McCoy's hands: Spock. He didn't need McCoy's almost soundless whisper, "He's in bad shape, Jim." He could sense the Vulcan's injuries; Spock's lighter frame had taken much more in the tank before he and Savaj had mastered the effect. Spock appeared to be in shock, and Savaj was barely on his own feet.

Kirk knelt down and lifted the unconscious Vulcan. His own ribs seemed to give way and he felt the veins pop out on his forehead. Spock was heavier than a Human of the same build would have been and Kirk supposed that in his own present shape he shouldn't have been able to get that weight off the ground. That, however, had nothing to do with the fact that he did it.

Then they were moving with Belen through the darkened laboratory and into some kind of tunnel. It was dark, too, and they communicated to each other mainly by touch. Kirk was to remember every step of the way as nightmare. McCoy tried to help him, but it was really a one-man job and McCoy was not up to it. Savaj was silent and seemed withdrawn.

Finally Belen triggered some door and they spilled out into light under a lavender sky. Kirk half fell into a mound of shattered crystal and took the moment to rest Spock's weight. The door closed with Belen still inside and he saw that they were under the overhang of some great ship—perhaps the one they had met in space near the planet. It filled the vast crater of the volcano. And everywhere canyons of thousand-foot crystal cliffs opened off the central core.

Kirk sank down for a moment, stopped. There was no way he could thread the maze from the other end to find the one opening they had come in from. They had no way to reach the *Enterprise*.

And if they could somehow find the way, the Designers would be after them at any moment, with all knowledge, all power. He could not move everything by his single will. Maybe the Vulcans had been right and there was some moment at which you had simply been overreached and should have the wit to know it. He did not feel as if he could get to his feet. Certainly not with the living weight he carried.

Then he did. He was prepared to strike out for whatever canyon until he dropped or they were caught.

He found Savaj indicating a direction. Kirk accepted

175

it. What Vulcans could calculate from astronomical positions or by some obscure orientation to the fields of a planet, he didn't want to know. They plunged into a canyon and moved.

"Jim," McCoy said. "You can't keep this up."

Kirk just shook his head.

Something gave way under his feet and he found himself sliding in an avalanche of crystal down a long slope toward a cliff edge. He couldn't get out of it.

Suddenly something caught both him and Spock and he realized that it was Savaj. The Vulcan was moving them somehow across and to the edge of the slide. Finally he caught a silver tree and stopped them on a ledge. McCoy had caught only the edge of the slide and it carried him near them.

Kirk saw Spock's eyes open. He didn't even try to explain what they were doing there. Nor did Spock ask. He gathered himself and attempted to stand. Kirk got a shoulder under him and helped him down to the floor of the canyon. He was helping Spock and he recognized the crystal canyon just inside the opening where they had come in from the ordinary hell of Helvan.

Kirk suddenly recognized the sense of *déjà vu*. It was the scene he had seen on the precognon in Trath's laboratory.

He caught Spock's eye. "We're home free, Spock!" Spock was able to stand now and Kirk slipped away for a moment to climb up on a rock by the cliff. "It's the entrance!"

He moved to slide the counterbalanced crystal sheet that closed it from the inside.

"Mr. Kirk, stop!"

It was Spock. Something in the tone cut through Kirk like a knife. He paused, but at his back was the knowledge that at any moment the Designers could be after them. Outside that sheet, feet away, the *Enterprise* would be keeping watch for their body signals and would beam them up home, where they could at least report.

And if Trath came for them then, perhaps it would only be for Kirk. There might even be some slim hope that Belen would have managed something that would let them all go free—if they moved *now*.

176

Spock couldn't know all the factors. Nor could he know Kirk's intent to go back, if he had to, to hold Trath to his bargain.

Kirk's hand was on the counterweight and he started to move it down.

"You *will* cease!" Spock said, and Kirk heard all of Vulcan behind it. If they got away, he would have to face that. He saw that also in Savaj's face behind Spock—all of Starfleet and all of Vulcan in one package. And still Kirk had to do what he had to do.

His hand froze on the counterweight and he had the sense of a rift in time in which he had time and eternity to recognize his own pattern, his own stake in it, his own blind spot.

Not once in all of this had he truly acceded to Spock's command. Nor did he yet see how he could have or could. The Vulcan would have been dead, would almost certainly die now—when one more defiance might keep him, and perhaps even the galaxy, safe. He saw the years when Spock had come out of his Vulcan box to yield to Kirk's command, even with that great Vulcan brain, even in moments when Kirk remained behind and ordered him off a disintegrating ship—or went to face a cloud-creature. Not once, even in what was essential to the Vulcan, had Kirk really laid down that weight of command and yielded, right or wrong, to the Vulcan's judgment. Had it been the knowledge that Kirk was in that box that was part of what had sent Spock off to Vulcan? Sooner or later some bullheadedness would get one or both of them killed. And if Kirk could not get out of his box, how could he expect Spock to get out of his, or Savaj—or even the Designers?

Yet Spock had managed it. And Savaj.

Kirk let the crystal sheet settle back into place. He jumped down from the rock to face Spock. "Yes, Captain," he said.

Spock saw the air begin to shimmer and knew what it was to which his decision had condemned them. They might have done better to take their chances in hell. He was yet surprised that Kirk had not.

Spock stepped forward to face Trath. He was in augmented command mode now, and the vibrations of Kirk's

177

resistance no longer hampered him. He drew strength from within and without.

The Designers shimmered into solidity: Trath, flanked by Flaem, Belen, and his fair colleague—and a small group behind them.

"The issue," Spock said to Trath, "has been resolved. Mr. Kirk is under my command. I do not yield him."

Trath turned to Kirk. "You were born to command, as I was, and you are responsible for the fate of a galaxy, as I for a universe. You are attempting to break a pattern that is born in your bones. It will not work. He does not command you. You are to keep your word, and I will keep mine."

Kirk stepped beside Spock. "It's true that the pattern is in my bones—as the Prometheus fault is, in me, and you. Our bones do not command us, nor our instincts, nor some unalterable doom. *We* command. We break patterns. We see through our blind spots. We steal the fire of the gods—only to find that we *are* gods. And if we are the vultures, too, that is our crime, our addiction, our misfortune—but it is not inalterable."

Trath shook his head. "We all live in Hell's Kitchen, subject Kirk, and we *like* it there—and it is indivisible from our greatness. There is no way out of that dilemma but surrender—the slow death of the spirit."

"Or of the body," Belen said very quietly.

Flaem lifted her head. "Better the fire."

"If that were the choice, perhaps," Spock said. "I speak as one who has attempted both the fire and the foreswearing of fire." He shook his head. "The design of the mechanism is also not built for retreat. There is no way out but forward."

Trath said, "I concur, subject V-Two. I do not deal in metaphysics or mercy. I am engaged in a war against a cancer that will consume the universe. And while I find your little lives attractive in some way, it is the lives of our children that concern me. I will use what I must. There is no practical answer to that. If I must bear a moral weight for the necessary, I will bear it."

"But," Kirk said suddenly, "the flaw in your design *is* a practical flaw." Kirk's face wore that look of arriving at a discovery. "Admiral Savaj," he said, "why does Vulcan not use animal life? Is it morality?"

"Vulcan does not distinguish the moral from the practical, Commander," Savaj said. "But the reason we do not use life is not morality but necessity. There is no great virtue in that necessity. When we had mastered some of our own aggression we were able to notice that the pain, rage, suffering of animals being used contaminated the psychic atmosphere and reinfected us with the passions of Hell's Kitchen. We cannot live in Hell's Kitchen. Not as what Vulcans have, at some cost, become."

"If you can't stand the heat, stay out of Hell's Kitchen," McCoy murmured. *"That's* why you didn't want Vulcans to serve on Human ships, isn't it? Not because of superiority or morality—"

"Most astute, Doctor," Savaj said. "It was, however, all three. Plus a certain concern for other species' fragility. Vulcans stand the heat extremely well. They merely become part of the hell."

McCoy nodded. "And the immediate galaxy cannot afford that luxury."

"Nor can the universe," Kirk said to Trath. "Don't you see? *That* is the flaw in your design. The practical flaw. Callousness breeds callousness. When you put other life in categories—self and Others, Designers and small life—we used to do it with black and white, this or that religion, Vulcan or Human, intelligent being or animal—that's when you can kill. If you can ever get the feeling that the other is *you*—a part of the self, the necessary-to-you, a sense of the oneness of All—then you can't. But the oneness exists, whether you know it or not, and the pain you cause returns to widen the breach of callousness in yourselves. You cannot heal the Prometheus fault by widening it in yourselves with the use of other lives."

Trath frowned. "You are saying we turn up the fire in Hell's Kitchen to our own destruction."

"I don't think you have the million years or whatever you think you have on your time scale. Unless you stop."

"Even if it were true, subject, we cannot give up the quest for greatness."

"No," Kirk said. He turned to Savaj. "That was your worry for Vulcan."

Savaj nodded. "We have counted the price well paid, or at least necessary to our survival. And yet there was a grandeur, a passion, perhaps a poetry to some of the an-

179

cient ways. The way of warrior brothers. The music of the far-rovers. The tragedies and the ecstasies. There is something that Spock did not find on Vulcan that he did find in the stars."

"What I found," Spock said, "is not merely Hell's Kitchen. Nor is it lost to Vulcan. You also have followed the path to the stars—so has my father in his way and others in theirs. And each of us has found some quest or some rapport that in the end we would choose above peace or freedom from pain."

"*S'haile* Savaj," Kirk said, "today you broke with the pattern of a lifetime. Vulcan does not lack for greatness."

Savaj returned the look, bowed his head fractionally. "Nor does Earth."

Kirk turned to Trath. "That has to be the answer. The quest, the striving, the personal bonds, the rapport you came to study—all those instincts that are for life, not against it. We can set those against the Promethean fault —and even use the fault itself to drive us to the stars, the dimensions. It can drive us to command and mastery and the power to smash through obstacles—but not flesh. Maybe it is even at the root of friendship. Animals who do not have individual clashes of aggressiveness do not form individual bonds. But also they know when to yield, and as a rule they do not kill."

Kirk took a step toward Trath. "There can be excitement enough in the universe without Hell's Kitchen. And greatness. And it may be that any small step to damp down the level of violence that feeds upon itself is finally the answer even to the dogs of war and the vultures of destruction." Kirk held out his hand to Trath.

Trath looked at him as if a puppy had offered to make peace. "Let us suppose that it were true, subject. I do not think that the breach of callousness would be much widened by the study of one little life. One that can conceive such an argument is worth further study. Will you give your little life to damp down the violence in your immediate galaxy?"

Kirk looked to Spock. "It is still a question. Do I have your permission, sir?"

"No, Mr. Kirk, you do not."

Kirk turned back to Trath. "My word was never mine to give. I am under his command."

For the first time Trath smiled. It was rather bitter as if he mocked not himself but some whole pattern that suddenly crumbled around him.

"Subject Kirk," he said, "there is an innocence that can make all things new. New life does not know what is impossible—and that may even be its virtue. It was one of the objects of this immediate study to determine whether your ship and your diverse selves, as a kind of microcosm of this galaxy, had or could develop a unique rapport and a capacity for breaking patterns. We recognize that the ultimate blind spot is the incapacity to break patterns in which one has a life invested—or perhaps even the lives of billions."

"You arranged for us to come, didn't you?" Kirk said. "Even down to Savaj?"

"The one mind that was able to detect our design? Of course. How could we fail to study that? We allowed him to select that which in his own mind was the best test of the Promethean question—yourselves."

"And the change of command?" Kirk asked.

"Essential, subject Kirk. That was *your* pattern."

"And if I had not broken it?"

"Then you would have been of little interest. I would have taken you, lest you escape the consequences of your actions, and closed down the experiment of this galaxy."

"*In* this galaxy?" McCoy asked.

"No. *Of,*" Trath answered.

"That's what I thought you said," McCoy said uneasily.

"But we did change," Kirk said. "Spock, Savaj, McCoy. Even Belen. Perhaps even Flaem—if it is true that for some moment you saw me as more than small life. And if even small lives can change and even Designers, then what remains impossible?" He stepped closer to Flaem and Belen, and for a moment Spock could sense him thinking his goodbyes across the gulf of what did remain impossible. Yet the impossible had existed for them and would not be forgotten. "In any case," Kirk said softly, "we have broken patterns together."

Spock stepped forward to meet Trath's eyes. "Blindness is not a condition of one man or one species. One can see farther, at times, through the eyes of others. One can learn from those who are struggling to be born. Change *your*

181

pattern. Give an end to callousness a chance—before it hastens your doom."

"Subject Spock," Trath said. "We are very old and you are very young. You have raised a practical flaw that we had not sufficiently considered. It remains to be seen whether that is, in truth, an insuperable flaw in our design. But your friend has correctly guessed why we have accelerated the experiment. Our recent evidence shows that we do not have the million years. Indeed there is more oneness between you and us than you could know. On our present course, the end of the All would have been reckoned within your lifetimes. Belen's solution—or the fire—was at hand. Or else a new experimental design. I do not promise an end to experiment. But I will give you this. For a time we will try the experiment on ourselves of healing the breach of callousness. And for suggesting that experiment, I will spare your friend—and your galaxy."

"Would you care to observe consequences?" Trath asked after a moment in which silent thought-farewells seemed to break down certain categories.

Trath turned and pointed his hand at the entrance to the canyon. The crystal sheet started to lift. The thousand-foot cliff above it started to shatter, falling down in lethal shards. The canyon started to shatter from that center. Trath touched a control and the Designers shimmered and disappeared.

Kirk looked at Spock, stricken. If he had disobeyed, he would have triggered their destruction.

Spock shrugged. "It was always their pattern, Mr. Kirk, to have maze within maze, trap within trap—and a certain finality to their tests."

The Designer shimmer started to form around them as the crystal cliffs of the whole valley crumbled in cataclysm. The Designer ship rose above them, departing.

Spock felt his consciousness dissolve—and reform on the bridge of the *Enterprise*.

Chapter Twenty-six

Kirk saw the shocked faces of the bridge crew and realized that the landing party was a pretty motley collection. Spock and Savaj were half naked and considerably the worse for wear, and Kirk and McCoy bore no resemblance to daisies either.

"Well," Kirk said. "Captain Spock, I have seen worse jobs of commanding a mission. On several occasions."

"So," Spock said, "have I. Including a certain usurpation of command in this one." He turned to survey Kirk. "Mr. Kirk, there remains a matter between us."

"I have never lost sight of that, sir." Kirk straightened to face the Vulcans. He had in fact done the unforgivable, and Vulcans were not noted for forgiveness. He had no concept at all of what the Vulcan penalty might be. And the fact that he had—belatedly—behaved himself would still not get him very far. Spock would say, properly, that he had several times risked his life, theirs, and the mission against Spock's orders.

"It is bound under Vulcan command code," Spock said, "and it is in other respects also beyond my recall. It is a matter of record with Starfleet and with Vulcan authorities—either or both of which can act on their own initiative."

Starfleet could, at a minimum, court-martial and ground him. What Vulcan authorities or Vulcans present could do he did not like to contemplate. And none of them were going to recognize pattern as a defense, or the ultimate breaking of pattern as extenuation.

"Of course," Savaj remarked thoughtfully, "the attempt to murder one's commanding officer and commanding admiral is, in some respects, even more serious than mutiny."

Kirk blinked. "But I was under the influence"— He stopped. "As a matter of fact," he said, looking at Savaj, "alien influences *have* been known to have a profound effect on starship personnel, up to and including many forms of aberrant behavior. Murder. Perhaps even mutiny."

"There is some precedent," Savaj said, "even in the record of this ship, for nonprosecution of aberrant behavior caused by alien influence—spores, viruses, and the like." He held Kirk's eyes. "If I am not mistaken, that has even included mutiny and the striking of a commanding officer before this trip."

Kirk rubbed his jaw absently. It had been some years and his jaw still remembered a Vulcan slap that had knocked him over a table,* and another occasion—when Kirk had baited Spock to drive out the spores and the Vulcan put a fist aimed at Kirk through a wall.**

"Yes," Spock said, "it has." He did not add that Kirk had taken it, and taken no action against him.

Spock looked at Kirk and Kirk saw that the anger had not dissipated. But it was becoming somewhat more personal.

Spock leaned over and pressed a button on the command seat. "Captain's Log. Judicial. Note is made of the fact that some members of the command crew have been under alien mind influence that made them act in manners impossible to their normal personalities and patterns. That demonstrably includes influence to attempt murder, and one could logically suppose that it could also include insubordination and mutiny. No official action is contemplated for such lapses, provided that they are not repeated."

He switched off and turned to Kirk. "Is that understood, Mr. Kirk?"

---

* "Star Trek" episode entitled "The Naked Time."
** "Star Trek" episode entitled "This Side of Paradise."

"Perfectly, Captain." He stood straight and let the relief and the gratitude show. It was not something Spock had to do, and they both knew that it was not wholly true. But it would serve.

"As for the matter between us," Spock said in the tone of not letting him off the hook. "I believe that can be resolved privately."

"Yes, sir."

"When you are quite recovered, you will conform to double fitness schedule and meet me for *asumi*—and chess."

"Yes, Captain Spock."

Spock did not smile. "That being the case, Mr. Kirk, and the Designers having departed, I am returning command of the *Enterprise* to you."

"What?" Kirk said.

"I believe you heard me, Captain Kirk."

"Yes, Mr. Spock." Kirk looked at Savaj.

"I have no objection, Captain. I believe the experience was salutary. But I have also perceived the beyond-level of which Mr. Spock spoke by which you do and can command him."

Kirk looked a question at Spock.

"I also have my pattern, Captain," Spock said, "and while I have occasionally despaired of you, you do have your moments. I will remember the one in which you broke your pattern. But I prefer, on the bridge, the one we set long ago." He gestured Kirk toward the center seat.

Kirk found himself smiling, also a little shaky, and he sat down in it.

Bones McCoy bounced on his heels at Kirk's left shoulder. "Now *that* feels right. You figure the Designers will keep their promise, Jim?"

"I figure," Kirk said, "that one of these million-year days we'll get the results of that experiment—if we haven't solved the problem ourselves first." He sat back in the chair. "And maybe we already *have*, on a day-to-day basis, one day at a time."

He looked at Savaj. All of them here belonged to difficult and dangerous species. Their solutions were partial and temporary and not always as careful of lives great and small as they might be. But he thought they were slowly wearing down the callousness and the categories that divided them.

He would not soon forget serving under Spock—and Savaj of Vulcan.

"Ahead Warp Factor Two," he said. Something seemed to settle back into place when he heard Sulu's, "Aye, Captain."

Epilogue

"Do you observe them in the precognon?" the fire-presence said.

"Dimly," the cool one answered. "It is difficult to predict those who are capable of reversing patterns."

"It is, however, fascinating," the flame one said. "I do not believe the promise said anything about visitation rights. . . ."

Glossary of Vulcan Terms

Asumi—Vulcan combat sport/dance.

K'asumi—The lethal all-out form of *asumi*. Never practiced except to the death.

K'vath—Enter, come, proceed.

Kavife—Challenge. Alternate grammatical form pertaining to the form and subject of the challenge.

Kolinahr—Advanced Vulcan discipline intended to achieve total logic by eliminating all emotions.

Le matya—Giant reptilian desert cat—roughly the *Tyrannosaurus rex* of Vulcan, but faster and smarter—and with poisonous claws and fangs.

S'haile—Title of profound respect pertaining to acknowledgment of a high level of personal accomplishment and commanding presence to which one would properly pay homage. The closest Terran translation would be the concept of a royalty that is not born but made —in fact, self-made. In that sense it might be rendered "Lord" by one who speaks as equal and as "My Lord" by one who does not.

Snarth—Quasi-intelligent mammalian predator of Vulcan.

T'hy'la*—friend, brother, lover.

---

* See note in *Star Trek—The Motion Picture, A Novel,* by Gene Roddenberry

T'hyvaj—Asumi empathic mirroring exercise first developed by ancient warrior-brothers on Vulcan.

T'Vareth—undisciplined cub, disobedient and subnormal whelp of an undesirable species. Not a term of endearment.

Tzaled—The ultimate Vulcan level of loyalty in which one takes responsibility for the well-being of the other even over his protests.

V'Kreeth—Name of a Vulcan ship and title given to its commander by Humans.

V'asumi—The sport/practice form of asumi in which strength may be restrained against a weaker opponent, but speed and skill must be used to train the other's full potential.

DOCTOR'S ORDERS

When Dr McCoy grumbles about the way the
Enterprise ought to be run, Captain Kirk
decides to leave the doctor in command while
he oversees a routine diplomatic mission. Kirk
beams down to a strange planet nicknamed
"Flyspeck" to negotiate its admission into
the Federation.

However, the doctor soon learns that command
is a double-edged sword when Kirk disappears
without a trace. McCoy comes under pressure
from Starfleet to resolve the situation
immediately. Matters go from bad to worse
when the Klingons arrive and stake their own
claim on Flyspeck.

Then another, more deadly power threatens
them all, and suddenly, Dr McCoy and the
Enterprise find themselves pitted against an
alien fleet in a battle they have no hope
of winning…

If you have difficulty obtaining any of the Titan range of books, you can order direct from Titan Books Mail Order, 71 New Oxford Street, London WC1A 1DG.
Tel: (01) 497 2150.

Star Trek novels 1 – 31	£2.95 each
Star Trek: The Next Generation novels 1 – 10	£2.95 each
Star Trek novels *32* onwards	£2.99 each
Next Generation novels 11 onwards	£2.99 each
Star Trek Giant novels 2 – 5	£3.95 each
Star Trek Giant novels 6 onwards	£3.99 each
Next Generation Giant novels	£3.99 each
The *Star Trek* Compendium	£8.95
Mr Scott's Guide to the Enterprise	£6.95
The *Star Trek* Interview Book	£5.95
Worlds of the Federation	£8.95
Captain's Log	£5.99

For postage & packing: on orders up to £5 add £1.20; orders up to £10 add £2.00; orders up to £15 add £2.50; orders up to £20 add £2.70; orders over £20 add £3.70. Make cheques or postal orders payable to Titan Books. NB. UK customers only.

While every effort is made to keep prices steady, Titan Books reserves the right to change cover prices at short notice from those listed here.